JOSÉ JOAQUÍN FERNÁNDEZ DE LIZARDI

Life and Deeds of the Famous Gentleman
Don Catrín de la Fachenda

JOSÉ JOAQUÍN FERNÁNDEZ DE LIZARDI

Life and Deeds of the Famous Gentleman Don Catrín de la Fachenda

ENGLISH TRANSLATION

EDITED BY

John Ochoa

TRANSLATED BY

Bonnie Loder

With notes by
Bonnie Loder and John Ochoa

The Modern Language Association of America
New York   2022

MLA and the MODERN LANGUAGE ASSOCIATION are trademarks owned by the Modern Language Association of America. For information about obtaining permission to reprint material from MLA book publications, send your request by mail (see address below) or e-mail (permissions@mla.org).

Library of Congress Cataloging-in-Publication Data

Names: Fernández de Lizardi, José Joaquín, 1776–1827, author. | Ochoa, John A. (John Andres), 1967– editor. | Loder, Bonnie, translator.
Title: Life and deeds of the famous gentleman Don Catrín de la Fachenda / José Joaquín Fernández de Lizardi ; edited by John Ochoa ; translated by Bonnie Loder.
Other titles: Vida y hechos del famoso caballero don Catrín de la Fachenda. English
Description: New York : The Modern Language Association of America, 2022.
Series: Texts and translations, 1079–2538 ; 37 | Includes bibliographical references. | Summary: "The first English translation of the picaresque novel by the Mexican author of El Periquillo Sarniento (The Itching Parrot). The main character is a rake, catrín (a dandy or fop), and criollo. The novel interrogates race and caste and political and social conditions in Latin America around 1810"—Provided by publisher.
Identifiers: LCCN 2021017756 (print) | LCCN 2021017757 (ebook) | ISBN 9781603295376 (paperback) | ISBN 9781603295383 (EPUB)
Classification: LCC PQ7297.F37 V513 2022 (print) | LCC PQ7297.F37 (ebook) | DDC 863/.5—dc23
LC record available at https://lccn.loc.gov/2021017756
LC ebook record available at https://lccn.loc.gov/2021017757

Texts and Translations 37
ISSN 1079-2538

Cover illustration: *El catrín*, by Lyouba Assadourova, from the series *Lotería Love44*.

Published by The Modern Language Association of America
85 Broad Street, Suite 500, New York, New York 10004-2434
www.mla.org

CONTENTS

ACKNOWLEDGMENTS

We would like to express our gratitude to James Hatch at the MLA for his faith in and patience with this project. At Penn State, Tom Beebee, Julia Cuervo-Hewitt, Giuli Dussias, and Sherry Roush provided guidance. Maria Izquierdo and Emily Wiggins assisted with the introduction, and the outside evaluators offered encouraging and constructive feedback. The work of the editorial team at the MLA, especially Susan Doose, Erika Suffern, and Zahra Brown, was essential.

A special thanks to Harold Fernández Cedeño for his careful editing and helpful suggestions regarding the translation.

—JO and BL

INTRODUCTION

José Joaquín Fernández de Lizardi (1776–1827) is a recognizable figure, an eighteenth-century intellectual, an Enlightenment man of letters. A member of the literate class, he received an early education consisting of Latin grammar, rhetoric, and some history and natural sciences. By profession he was what could today be called an op-ed journalist and a social critic. Lizardi, a great follower of French political ideas and intellectual tendencies of his time, was invested in innovative concepts such as universal democracy, the social contract, and the natural rights of man. His pseudonym was "El pensador mexicano" ("the Mexican thinker"), a direct reference to the radical French philosopher Jean-Jacques Rousseau.

Lizardi's journalism, his opinions, and his fiction reflect the thinking of an idealist, albeit a somewhat cynical one. Lizardi believed in equality before the law, though his views were not quite as extreme as those of other revolutionaries of the time. But he also harbored a healthy skepticism about the ability of powerful institutions, such as the church and the aristocracy, to see to that equality, especially in the American colonies.

Perhaps a better nickname for Lizardi would have been "the teacher." Although his ideas and politics evolved throughout his life, his faith in education remained constant. He trusted that the systematic acquisition of information afforded by universal literacy would elevate the masses and make all citizens more responsible. He trusted that knowledge would result in democracy and maintained that the role of intellectuals like him was to serve as educators of the masses.

In addition to a number of short articles, Lizardi wrote more extensive works in the picaresque genre, a well-known form at the time. His novel *El Periquillo Sarniento* (*The Itching Parrot*), published in installments between 1816 and 1831—mostly because his main source of income was from broadsheet periodicals and not books, which were more costly to produce—is frequently labeled the first Latin American novel. The picaresque, a genre that started in Spain with *Lazarillo de Tormes* in 1554, features a young antihero whose difficult life keeps him constantly on the move from one painful circumstance to another—he often mixes with outcasts, criminals, and other marginal figures. But despite the many adversities he encounters, he always manages to survive by his wits.

The picaresque remained popular for centuries and produced many notable examples and, as is to be expected with any long-lived genre, it gradually evolved. When Lizardi wrote his own version of a picaresque novel, he no longer followed the original Spanish model of *Lazarillo* but imitated more recent European models such as *Gil Blas de Santillane* (1715–35), by the French writer Alain-René Lesage. Lesage's variety of picaresque is no longer as cynical as the Spanish sources, and his tone is lighter.

As the cultural historian Christopher B. Conway illustrates, Mexico City at the end of the colonial era—the natural habitat of Lizardi's protagonists—was an ideal setting for a picaresque life (23–53). For hundreds of years, Mexico had been one of the Spanish Empire's most valuable overseas possessions. However, at the time when Lizardi wrote, the empire was in full decline and on the verge of collapse. With the example of the newly independent nation of the United States hanging in the air, Mexico was about to declare its own independence, along with the rest of the Spanish colonies on the American continent.

The Kingdom of New Spain, as Mexico was then known, had a refined viceregal court and a complex culture maintained by its vast resources, especially precious metals such as silver. Yet despite this relative prosperity there were numerous internal social tensions and massive racial inequality. Since the initial Spanish conquest during the sixteenth century, the indigenous population had been ruled by a white, Spanish minority—but this white minority was itself divided. The most important administrative positions at the top of the hierarchy were reserved for the newly arrived *peninsulares*, those Spaniards born in Spain. These individuals occupied key positions in the government bureaucracies, in the church, and in the commercial monopolies and trade guilds. But these Spanish newcomers' children and grandchildren, born in the New World and part of the same dominant Spanish culture, were known as *criollos* and were automatically relegated to a secondary status. Although *criollos* were well-off compared to most of the country's inhabitants, their possibilities for advancement were limited. The top jobs were always reserved for recent arrivals from the Continent. Naturally, the *criollos* resented both the situation and the newcomers, whom they contemptuously called *gachupines*.[1]

By the time Lizardi began practicing his craft at the beginning of the nineteenth century, the *criollos* had built up centuries of resentment. As important and volatile as it was, though, this resentment in the upper echelons of the population was eclipsed by a much larger division within the rest of the population. The vast majority of Mexicans, then as today, were *mestizos*, or persons of mixed Indian and European ancestry.[2] Indians and Africans of unmixed ancestry also constituted significant minorities. A rigid caste system maintained the dividing lines between these populations.

An artistic genre known as *cuadros de castas* ("caste paintings") vividly illustrates the various sectors of society with what was then considered scientific precision (figs. 1–3). This type of painting was practiced by artists with an academic training and was carried out in the scientific spirit of the Enlightenment, with a style informed by the classificatory advancements of the Swedish botanist Charles Linnaeus, who organized all living beings into logical categories (family, gender, order, etc.). Throughout the eighteenth century, as the historian Barbara Maria Stafford points out, nature art (still lifes, landscapes, zoological and botanical illustrations) often reflected the influence of steady scientific development.

In this scientific spirit, the *cuadros de castas* were intended to register social truth in almost ecological terms, with a supposedly neutral eye. The objective was to instruct the population about the implications of interracial couplings and the

Figure 1. Miguel Cabrera. *De español y albina, tornatrás (From Spaniard and Albino Woman, Turnback)*. 1763. Oil on canvas. Private collection.

Figure 2.
Miguel Cabrera. *De
español y tornatrás,
tente-en-el-aire*
(*From Spaniard and
Turnback, Hang-in-
the-Air*). 1763. Oil
on canvas. Private
collection.

Figure 3.
Miguel Cabrera.
*De español e india,
nace mestiza (From
Spaniard and Indian
Is Born a Mestiza).*
1763. Oil on canvas.
Private collection.

products thereof, as the art historian Ilona Katzew has documented. The paintings were exhibited in public places to reinforce the idea that social and racial hierarchies existed naturally.

At first glance, it may seem as though the sets of parents and children depicted in these paintings are presented in a neutral, unbiased light. However, the fiction that the categories to which they belonged were a product of nature and not the result of cultural prejudice is undermined by one remarkable element: the paintings include textual inscriptions listing the commonly used terms for persons of mixed race—and these terms were certainly not neutral. Some simply sound odd to the modern reader, but others are cruel and degrading, even dehumanizing. Terms such as *tornatrás* ("turnback") and *tente-en-el-aire* ("hang-in-the-air") were clearly born of prejudice.

The same scientific spirit that seems to inspire these curious paintings also motivated a European observer to look at Mexico during this period. The great German naturalist and traveler Alexander von Humboldt lived there from 1803 to 1804. On returning to Europe he published a very statistical, supposedly neutral scientific report on the economy, resources, and institutional aspects of places he had visited. His influential *Political Essay on the Kingdom of New Spain* (*Essai politique sur le royaume de la Nouvelle Espagne*) is full of measurements and tables but doesn't give many explicit details about the racial inequalities that shaped social conditions in Mexico. Still, Humboldt was a good scientist and a good eyewitness. He briefly mentions the street life he saw in Mexico City, describing a city full of vendors, shopkeepers, muleteers, and day laborers. He notes "twenty to thirty thousand wretches (*Saragates, Guachinangos*) of whom the greatest number pass the night *sub dio*," or sleeping outdoors

(*Political Essay* 1: 235). *Saragates* ("rogues") and *guachinangos* ("red snapper fish") are exactly the sort of racial street terms that we find recorded in the *cuadros de castas*, and they speak to a harsh, hierarchical reality.

We find evidence of this rigid caste system in Lizardi's fiction. In his first picaresque novel, *El Periquillo Sarniento*, the *criollo* protagonist arrives in jail to discover that, "[p]or mi desgracia, entre tanto hijo de su madre como estaba encerrado en aquel sótano, no había otro blanco más que yo, pues todos eran indios, negros, lobos, mulatos y castas, motivo suficiente para ser en la realidad, como fui, el blanco de sus pesadas burlas" ("to my misfortune, every other mother's son was locked in that dungeon, and there was no other white besides me, because they were all Indians, blacks, *lobos* [wolves], mulattos, and other specimens of the castes. And this was reason enough for me to become the *blanco* of their heavy gibes"; 424; my trans.)—a pun, since *blanco* means both "white" and "target" or "bullseye." Much like Don Catrín, this character is a pompous member of his class who is initially horrified by being forced in with these "inferior" members of society. But this young innocent quickly learns the ways of the rabble and is soon cursing, gambling, and taking advantage of others, like any good picaresque criminal.

In the picaresque story *Don Catrín de la Fachenda*, here translated into English for the first time, Lizardi offers a complicated view of the firmly established racial system in Mexico. The protagonist, another *criollo* whose family has fallen on hard times, also happens to be a self-declared *catrín*, a "dandy" or "fop." But Lizardi characterizes his status as *catrín* as if it were a racial class, just another caste.

As is often the case with any fixed forms of social stratification, the lower the position of a caste, the fewer prospects there are for advancement. Those of the lower classes have little hope of rising to a higher class. In Mexico at the beginning of the nineteenth century, when Lizardi wrote his novels, this inequality had reached a breaking point, an inevitable situation that was only accelerated by the tumultuous political events in Europe brought about by the Napoleonic Wars. Napoleon had invaded Spain in 1808 and installed his brother Joseph as king. The British sent an expeditionary force under the Duke of Wellington to the Peninsula to assist with the resistance. An international proxy war began in all Spanish territories. But previously existing political divisions within Spain resulted in various foreign-aligned factions, and the war became both internal and external. These factions represented different ideologies, and each sought opposite outcomes for Spain.

Given this complicated situation in Spain, the colonial territories naturally fell into disarray. In America, the resentful *criollos* saw an opportunity to address their long-standing grievances. Important questions arose for this class: Should they rebel against King Joseph, puppet king of the French? If so, in favor of whom? Would they declare allegiance to the rebel liberal parliament, the anti-monarchist *Cortes de Cádiz*? (This democratic congress was willing to grant the colonies equal representation if they won.) Or should the *criollos* declare total independence from Europe, as the United States had done thirty years prior? And if so, from which form of government would they declare their independence?

Around 1810, when insurrections began throughout what would become Latin America, some *criollos* tried to have it both ways, according to the historian D. A. Brading (562–67). They rose up in arms, pledging allegiance to the deposed Bourbon monarchy, because they saw this as an opportunity to put an end to the longtime domination of the recently ar-

rived *peninsulares,* who in turn had had to remain faithful—
whether they liked it or not—to Joseph Bonaparte, nominal
head of the Spanish overseas administration. By declaring fi-
delity to the deposed king, Ferdinand VII, these rebel *criollos*
conveniently claimed that the conflict in Europe had forced
their hand, and that they had been compelled to separate
themselves from the French-imposed government in order
to support the legitimate Spanish monarchy. Other *criollos*
sought independence in order to establish the vanguard of
Spanish liberalism. Still others declared independence in a
spirit of pure Americanism, with the intention of founding
new nations.

In Mexico, the dispute at the top of the caste system between *criollos* and *peninsulares* sparked a long-simmering
class-and-race war across the entire population. The situation reached a flash point in September 1810, owing to the efforts of a provincial *criollo* priest, Miguel Hidalgo y Costilla.
Today celebrated as Mexico's founding father, Father Hidalgo was an ingenious individual who had experimented,
and failed, at several somewhat exotic agricultural projects
(those involving Asian silkworms, old-world mulberry trees
to feed the silkworms, and innovative forms of beekeeping).
Hidalgo was also a political experimenter. An avid reader
of the forbidden works of the radical French thinkers, he
was associated with a club—a literary circle with Masonic
sympathies, considered heretical by the church—consisting of provincial intellectuals who shared his inclinations.
Father Hidalgo had long been using his church pulpit to
rouse the class consciousness of the *mestizo* and indigenous
congregants of his parish, something that had kept him relegated to the relatively obscure provinces. By 1810 he was
convinced that the time was ripe for revolution. Fearing that

the authorities were on their way to arrest him, on the night of 16 September he rang the bell of his church and called on his parishioners to rise up in arms.[3]

This sudden birth of the Mexican nation contains a world of contradictions: a white, *criollo* priest—an agent of the highest religious authority—calling on the vast *mestizo* and Indian underclasses to rise in arms against white *criollos* like himself. Like most of Hidalgo's experiments, this one did not go well for him. He was soon captured and beheaded by the colonial authorities. But the fight continued, lasting a full decade until the exhausted Spanish government finally withdrew in 1821, granting Mexico its independence.

The plot of *Don Catrín de la Fachenda* takes place during the years immediately preceding Mexico's war of independence and was probably written as hostilities were taking place. But curiously, there is no direct mention of the war in the novel. Possible explanations for this include the author's own political ambivalence toward the momentous events swirling around him. In spite of this great omission the book is deeply concerned with the conditions that produced the conflict, and it offers a vivid representation of the circumstances, including the social and political frictions, that sparked Mexico's war of independence.

The Story of a Story

Don Catrín de la Fachenda was Lizardi's last book and was published posthumously in 1832. *Don Catrín* shares many traits with the author's previous novel, *El Periquillo*, but there are some key differences. *Don Catrín* is much shorter and lesser known. That said, it is in many ways a better book. It is more challenging, both morally and intellectually, and it is quite arguably funnier.

The choice of the picaresque genre as the means for Lizardi's social critique makes good sense. In an important study on modern national identity, *Imagined Communities*, Benedict Anderson uses the picaresque as a case study to explore the rise of national identity during the early nineteenth century. According to Anderson, the social fluidity of the *pícaro*, or rogue, offers a way of penetrating the supposedly impassable layers of a society (29–30). The picaresque, Anderson contends, is an ideal vehicle for surveying the long-term, negative effects of colonialism on a newly forming nation such as Mexico (29). According to Anderson, the marks of colonialism—what the philosopher Michel Foucault called the "institutions of power," meaning both the agents and the subjects of that power—were the "hospitals, prisons, remote villages, monasteries, Indians, Negroes" (30). Lizardi's main characters become quite familiar with each of these.

These rakish *pícaro* protagonists take inventory of their crude surroundings and the denizens thereof, noticing what belongs where and to whom—even if they do so only to see what they can steal or somehow use to their benefit. The *pícaro*'s acquisitive, if wary, vision highlights the "institutions of power" that are in turn trying to keep an eye on, and discipline, him. These institutions, normally invisible due to their very everydayness, are certainly not invisible to him. In his wanderings, the *pícaro* also skirts the underworld, a place very much part of the real world but rarely seen in more genteel forms of art and literature.

Besides being a standard *pícaro*, the protagonist of Lizardi's novel is also a *catrín*, a term that requires some explanation. A *catrín* is a fixture that exists to this day in the popular imagination of Mexico. The *Diccionario de americanismos* (*Dictionary of Americanisms*) defines a *catrín* as someone "que muestra elegancia en el vestir y esmero en

Figure 4. José Guadalupe Posada. *La calavera catrina* (*The Elegant Skull*). Ca. 1910. Public domain.

el cuidado de su persona" ("who shows elegance in their dress, and great effort in their personal care"; "Catrín, -na"; my trans.). The Mexican game of chance called *lotería* ("lottery"), a kind of pictographic bingo, has an image of a *catrín* among its picture cards from the early twentieth century (see the artist's rendering on the cover of this volume). Another example comes from the late-nineteenth-century artist and political cartoonist José Guadalupe Posada, who created a character meant to satirize the pretensions of the privileged class of the time. This character was known as *la catrina*, the female *catrín* (fig. 4).

Lizardi's protagonist Don Catrín de la Fachenda is three things at once: a rakish *pícaro* in the tradition of the picaresque; a *catrín*, a dandy or fop; and a *criollo*, a person born in the New World and belonging to the same dominant class as their Spanish-born parents but relegated to a secondary status. As the character himself tells it, he comes from a racially unmixed family that has fallen on hard times. His father pleads with him in vain to stay honest and does his best to help his son maintain a sense of bourgeois respectability. He tries first to give his son an education that will lead him to the professions, like the law and soldiering. When that fails, he tries apprenticeships in various trades. But Don Catrín will have none of it, since he has an active dislike for work and an undue sense of entitlement, thinks most physical labor is beneath him, and is also rather stubborn and a bit dumb to boot.

Don Catrín attempts to justify this sense of entitlement with frequent rants about what and who he is. At the beginning of the narrative, he announces with pride that he descends from the "raza," or "race," of the *catrines*. When he runs into another *catrín*, a swindler in full swing, the pair marvel at having run across a "nuevo pariente" ("new family member") of the "misma raza" ("same race"; ch. 6). Since when are dandies—*catrines*—related by blood?

By questioning the nature of this person who exerts "great effort in their personal care," the novel also questions what it means to be born into a social class. In doing so, *Don Catrín* challenges the notion of racial essentialism and the validity of hereditary rights. But it also raises doubts about the power of the individual will: what does it take to make something of oneself, to smarten up, and thus to become somebody?

In brief, the novel pits two important notions, self-determination and fate, against each other. Although Don Catrín makes much of his lineage as a *catrín*—his inherited characteristics—at the same time he behaves like a self-made *catrín*: someone who dresses like, acts like, aspires to be, and finally becomes someone else. In this way, *Don Catrín* racializes the performative identity of both the *pícaro* and the *catrín*. This double reference to both the *pícaro* and the *catrín* is magnified as Don Catrín descends to the depths of society and becomes a hardened criminal. The novel intentionally confuses categories that are generally considered innate and thus cannot be chosen, like race and caste, with deliberate behavioral choices, such as attention to appearance, social disguise, and a life of crime.

In another famous novel about the strength of the individual will, Daniel Defoe's *Robinson Crusoe* (1719), the young protagonist has a deep desire to escape from what he considers his inevitable but boring destiny: a respectable life within the middle class, what his father calls the "middle station" (6–7). To avoid this inevitability, he takes to the sea in search of adventure. Ironically, when he is shipwrecked on an island, he ends up reconstructing in detail the very materialistic "middle station" he was fleeing. He builds a walled mansion, plants a plot of land, and secures a personal servant.

Likewise, Don Catrín's announced intention is to leave behind the social and racial strictures of his situation as a respectable *criollo* because he feels he does not belong there. Much later he even destroys his *ejecutorias*, the letters patent that prove his lineage, and renounces "toda cosa que oliera a nobleza" ("everything that smelled faintly of nobility"), thereby rejecting any connection to his class (ch. 11). Don Catrín does this out of anger at not being treated better in jail. As a result, however, he is better able to fit in with the "pillos" ("common thieves") with whom he has been running for quite some time (ch. 11). This final rejection will make him not only a better *pícaro* but also a better *catrín*. In this way, he seems ultimately to abandon the concept of *catrín* as an inherited condition in favor of the *catrín* as an actor, but when he praises what he believes to be the virtue of *catrines*, it is not always clear which of the two senses he means to invoke.

Conventional *catrines* are chameleons. Curiously, however, when Don Catrín disguises himself, he does so to pass as a member of the affluent class he has recently left behind. Every time he comes into some money, he goes to the secondhand markets to reconstruct his previous appearance. On one occasion he purchases "dos camisas de coco, un frac muy razonable y todo lo necesario para el adorno de mi persona, sin olvidárseme el reloj, la varita, el tocador, los peines, la pomada, el anteojo y los guantes, pues todo esto hace gran falta a los caballeros de mi clase" ("two percale shirts, a very reasonable tailcoat, and all the items necessary for the adornment of my person, without forgetting the watch, little cane, powders, combs, creams, monocle, and gloves, for all this is indispensable to gentlemen of my class"; ch. 7). Then, when he inevitably loses everything again, he is forced to sell his trappings and ends up dressed in rags, hanging around in places and doing things not befitting a *criollo* of his class.

Don Catrín's frequent reentering and reexiting of his original social class exposes the idea that membership in this class is an empty distinction. This idea is evident even before his decision to abandon his standing and embark on a criminal life. His family is proud of much, but has nothing, at least in material terms. It could be said that Don Catrín comes from nothing, and although he is in fact no longer anyone, he remains a proud blue blood and claims to be a lot—but his lot comes and goes.

Whatever Don Catrín has or doesn't have, whatever he is or is not, he puts on a good show—and the show is what really counts. It offers an excellent vantage point for looking at the foundations—both stable and unstable—that organized and upheld the social hierarchies at that particular, and explosive, moment in Mexican history.

A Matter of History

That unique moment in Mexican history—between 1810 and 1821—is when most of the Latin American wars of independence erupted. Although the issue of independence is not explicitly addressed in *Don Catrín de la Fachenda*, the book engages with the complexities of independence and its effects on political, moral, and social systems. The early-nineteenth-century reader of this novel, who encounters Don Catrín's efforts to define himself and declare his personal independence, is invited to consider the analogous struggles happening at the national level. Similar questions can be asked about both the character of Don Catrín and the Mexican nation itself: Is it possible to free oneself from one's origins, from genealogy, from an inherited but stifling situation? Is it possible to act with true independence, to exert free will?

It is difficult to find a clear and consistent position in Lizardi's work regarding his own *criollo* class. Some scholars see in his work an effort to consolidate his class, a "desire to build a solid bourgeois home for the *criollo*," as Antonio Benítez-Rojo puts it (338). For Benítez-Rojo, ridiculous picaresque criminals such as Don Catrín and Periquillo exist to "correct the moral defects he [Lizardi] saw among the middle-class *criollos*" (331).

The complexities of this novel demand more than a simple reading, especially if we take into account the monumental political and social changes happening at the time. When reading this book, one must keep in mind two related questions: Why did Lizardi decide to avoid any explicit representation of the Mexican War of Independence? And why did he resort to this quirky version of the humorous picaresque, full of windy digressions and double entendres, to deliver his sharp critiques?

It is worth returning to another observer of Mexico of the time, namely Humboldt. Like Lizardi's novel, Humboldt's work was meant to give an honest reckoning of the real conditions in New Spain (although Humboldt's readers were the educated European elites, not the Mexican locals). Humboldt published elegant works of illustrated travel literature, with titles such as *Vues des Cordillères et monumens des peuples indigènes de L'Amérique* (*Views of the Cordilleras and Monuments of the Indigenous Peoples of the Americas*).[4] The natural wonders and the ruins of the vanished pre-Columbian civilizations are attractively framed in this work, whose expensive engravings reveal vast landscapes of fertile lands, high mountains, and volcanoes, as well as pyramids and archaeological findings, hieroglyphs, sculptures, and a few museum objects.

On the whole, however, Humboldt includes very little about the current, and wretched, conditions of the Indians and of the lower castes more generally. This omission is significant. It conveys a political subtext that amounts to a subtle moral condemnation, suggesting that everything good and rich in Mexico, like the ancient civilizations, had been either mismanaged and ruined or, like the impressive natural landscape and resources, was yet to be profitably exploited. The implicit criticism is that Spain had not been good for Mexico. Of course, Humboldt could not express this anti-imperialist opinion directly. His trip had happened at the invitation of the Spanish Crown, which had generously provided him with unprecedented access to its colonial possessions—especially unprecedented for someone like him, a Protestant representative of liberal Europe. Humboldt had been commissioned to give shining accounts of Spain's American possessions and to offer a glowing inventory of the greatness of Mexico. And Humboldt does indeed observe everything—except colonial oppression. But it is there, conspicuous in its absence.

Lizardi's mission to give an honest account of his country's political and social situation was equally constrained. At the beginning of the nineteenth century, when he was still a young writer, Spain's Bourbon government had recently begun to soften press censorship as part of its modernizing reforms, the goal being to avoid possible uprisings. The first daily newspaper of New Spain, the *Diario de México* (*Newspaper of Mexico*), had begun its run in 1805. One result of this carefully managed liberalization was that Lizardi and other intellectuals began to make a living through their writings. The occasional broadsheet appeared, discussing some problem of the day. However, once the dispute or controversy that prompted the broadsheet died down, the publication vanished; sometimes the government suppressed it. For the writers behind these publications, this was a tenuous existence.

Clearly, the Bourbon government's controlled relaxation of censorship did not mean carte blanche had been extended or that absolute freedom of self-expression had been granted. Lizardi often had to keep silent on important matters, or to limit his commentary to indirection and allegory. Occasionally he miscalculated and, as a result, spent some time behind bars.

It was this early taste of freedom of expression that would shape Lizardi's entire career. In all his work we find a firm belief in the future of his homeland, though this belief is also marked by a certain reticence, a skepticism about whether radical change will actually come; there is a cynical thread that runs through his writing. At the same time, Lizardi never quite overcame the sense that he needed to moderate his voice and maintain a certain discretion in expressing his opinions.

In addition to the pressures of censorship, Lizardi would also have been under serious financial pressure. His reading, and purchasing, public was limited, capricious, unaccustomed to political sincerities, and not always interested in paying to read about controversies that did not directly affect them. In short, his colonial *criollo* audience had to be courted and entertained. Lizardi could not afford to infuriate or offend with too much directness. When he wrote his social satires or humorous didactic dialogues about matters of public interest, or expressed political opinions, he had to captivate, or at least entertain, before he could hope to teach or denounce. He had to draw his readers in with things and sounds they knew. This is why in his writings we often hear voices that would be familiar to his readers, such as the voice of the local priest with his pedantic Sunday sermons, someone so familiar that it would perhaps be soothing to find him in print. At other times Lizardi resorts to crude, popular language and humor one would hear on the streets. His own authorial voice always had to present itself indirectly, disguised as something that it was not necessarily groomed to be—much like a *catrín*.

Lizardi's political and social opinions shifted throughout his life, a fact he was likely aware of. Written toward the end of his life, *Don Catrín* reflects the author's later political stances. Lizardi began his career as a young writer living in a highly structured viceregal society; the end of his life and career witnessed a newly independent but chaotic republic where class and racial allegiances had just been shattered.

Although it is somewhat difficult to emphasize how important independence is within a novel that does not explicitly address it, Mexico's independence undeniably affected the author's entire existence. The war and the first years of the new republic must have been disconcerting and alarming to him. When the Spanish government withdrew in 1821, it left a power vacuum that led to decades of continuous bloodshed. In the 1820s, a self-proclaimed emperor, Agustín de Iturbide, rose and fell. Soon after came a series of leaders whose politics reflected an archetype dominant in nineteenth-century Latin America: the *caudillo*, or populist strongman. Foremost among these was the megalomaniac general Antonio López de Santa Anna, who more than once rose to absolute power.

Postindependence Mexico was beset by a series of disasters and farcical tragicomedies. Ridiculous foreign interventions occurred; one, known as the *Guerra de los pasteles*, or Pastry War, was initiated in part by damages caused to a French bakery during a riot. When, like Don Catrín, the dictator Santa Anna lost a leg during his misadventures, he had it buried with a full state funeral. Later, Santa Anna lost an even more important limb, a third of Mexico's territory, which he ceded to the United States during the latter's aggressive war of expansion. Mexico, caught in a debilitating struggle between liberals and conservatives, would default on its foreign debt and would be seized by European creditors during the 1860s, resulting in a painful occupation by the French. Yet in the midst of all this chaos, some truly notable achievements stand out: slavery was abolished; a profoundly modern federal constitution was created in 1857, protecting individual rights and emphasizing the separation of powers; and Benito Juárez became the first indigenous president of any nation on the American continent.

The worldview of *Don Catrín de la Fachenda*, both ridiculous and profoundly serious and promising, foreshadows this immediate national future. The novel's complexities transcend simplistic, comic criminality; crude humor; and moralizing, pompous sermons of questionable irony. Its hybrid main character—at once a *pícaro*, a *catrín*, and a *criollo*—embodies this complexity.

Any attempt to define with any sort of specificity what it means to be a *catrín* simply cannot account for the complexity. At one point, Don Catrín offers a list of rules, which he falsely attributes to Machiavelli, for aspiring *catrines* to follow:

1. Treat everyone pleasantly, but love no one.
2. Be very liberal in granting honors and titles, and flatter everyone.
3. If you manage to land a good position, serve only the powerful.
4. Howl with the wolves. That is, assume the character that works to your best advantage, even if it is most criminal.
5. If you hear someone lie in your favor, confirm his lie with a nod.
6. If you have done something that you do not wish to acknowledge, deny it.
7. Etch all injuries done unto you in stone, and any kindnesses in dust.
8. If you deceive someone, deceive him to the very end, for you have no need of his friendship.
9. Promise much and do little.
10. Be your own fellow man, and do not concern yourself with others.

(ch. 9)

This list clearly pokes fun at the aphorisms of eighteenth-century writers such as Voltaire, Samuel Johnson, and Benjamin Franklin. But some of these rules also display practical ethics, even a kind of wisdom. Recalling the Aristotelian notion of *phronesis* ("practical wisdom"), they also point to Rousseau's two concepts of self-love, *amour de soi* and *amour propre*, in his *Discourse on the Origins of Inequality* (*Discours sur l'origine et les fondements de l'inégalité*, 1755)—prerequisites for any human being to exist responsibly within society. The individual must fulfill these obligations to himself before being able to function as an effective part of the community and thus before being able to join the collective social contract. But Don Catrín's list also stresses the contradictions that result when Rousseau's concept of self-love turns into selfishness and social responsibility becomes murky. This murkiness is emblematic of the historical and social landscape of Lizardi's novel, a world in which the ridiculous coexists with the serious, the heroic with the clueless, the selfish with the selfless.

Don Catrín's identity as a *catrín*, which he both performs and suffers from, magnifies his observations about the institutions of power he encounters in his wanderings among those who live under the yoke of these institutions. Recall Anderson's observation that because of their free-floating qualities, *pícaros* make exceptional societal witnesses, firsthand observers of abuse and excess. One could say that Don Catrín is an even more exceptional witness, because this *pícaro* is also a *catrín* who wanders the margins of society, looking for opportunities, casing out the valuable, playing the angles. The *catrín*, with his unique demeanor and attire, uses his powers of imitation and disguise to lose himself in the crowd: he is an excellent reader of social situations and patterns. And when he sneaks into places where he doesn't belong, his simulations offer a kind of *cuadros de castas*, exaggerated representations of the standing hierarchies.

Don Catrín is a silly character, and the dilemmas and moral challenges he encounters frequently lead him to contradictory responses, as Nicolas Shumway notes (365–66). As narrator, Don Catrín always justifies his own missteps with arrogant explanations, yet rarely does he recognize them as mistakes. Because this evasive scoundrel is positioned as a witness to a complex world that is becoming more complicated every day, he never realizes the implications and effects of his actions. But the book itself does. Don Catrín's antics highlight the dramatic conditions and events of the newly formed Mexican nation, circa 1810, whose birth is explicitly absent in this narrative but at the same time burns within it. This contradiction demands that both Don Catrín and his contemporary reader form their own opinions about what is right and wrong.

Notes

1. A somewhat dated but still very readable history of Mexico is Leslie Byrd Simpson's *Many Mexicos*. See in particular Simpson's chapters on the late colonial period (130–220).

2. We use the term *Indian* advisedly, echoing its common usage in Latin America, where it is not necessarily pejorative. There the term is just as charged as it is in the United States, but in Latin America it is more polyvalent. Plenty of writers and intellectuals, many of them Indians themselves arguing on the side of indigenous rights and identity, employ the term. *American Indian* and *Native American* are not accurate substitutions for referring to the many indigenous people of what is now Latin America, since these terms are US-centric.

3. An engaging account of the insurrection can be found in Simpson (209–25).

4. This is an elegantly hand-colored set of engraved images, printed in large folio, and available by subscription only. Such luxury items were necessary for Humboldt to fund his subsequent trips.

Works Cited

Anderson, Benedict. *Imagined Communities*. Verso, 1991.

Benítez-Rojo, Antonio. "José Joaquín Fernández de Lizardi and the Emergence of the Spanish American Novel as National Project." *Modern Language Quarterly*, vol. 57, no. 2, 1996, pp. 325–39.

Brading, D. A. *The First Americans*. Cambridge UP, 1991.

"Catrín, -na." *Diccionario de americanismos*, Asociación de Academias de la Lengua Española, 2016, lema.rae.es/damer/?key=catrin.

Conway, Christopher B. *Nineteenth-Century Spanish America: A Cultural History*. Vanderbilt UP, 2015.

Defoe, Daniel. *Robinson Crusoe*. Edited by Michael Shinagel, W. W. Norton, 1975.

Fernández de Lizardi, José Joaquín. *El Periquillo Sarniento*. Edited by Carmen Ruiz Barrionuevo, Cátedra, 1997.

Humboldt, Alexander. *Political Essay on the Kingdom of New Spain*. Translated by John Black, Longman, Hurst, Rees, Orme, and Brown, 1811. 4 vols.

———. *Vues des Cordillères et monumens des peuples indigènes de L'Amérique*. F. Schoell, 1810.

Katzew, Ilona. *Casta Painting: Images of Race in Eighteenth-Century Mexico*. Yale UP, 2004.

Rousseau, Jean-Jacques. *Discourse on the Origins of Inequality (Second Discourse), Polemics, and Political Economy*. Translated by Judith R. Bush et al., edited by Roger D. Masters and Christopher Kelly, UP of New England, 1992. Collected Writings of Rousseau.

Shumway, Nicolas. "*Don Catrín de la Fachenda* and Lizardi's Crisis of Moral Authority." *Revista de Estudios Hispánicos*, vol. 30, no. 3, 1996, pp. 361–74.

Simpson, Leslie Byrd. *Many Mexicos*. 4th ed., U of California P, 1966.

Stafford, Barbara Maria. *Voyage into Substance: Art, Science, Nature, and the Illustrated Travel Account, 1760–1840*. MIT Press, 1984.

NOTE ON THE TRANSLATION

My aim in this translation has been to produce a reading that transmits the elements of orality, linguistic experimentation, irony, and humor so fundamental to the novel and to convey as much as possible to foreign audiences the story's complex portrait of Lizardi's Mexico. Language is key to appreciating the paradoxes embodied by the narrator, who is at once cunningly resourceful and idiotically foolish, and also to appreciating the myriad linguistic, cultural, and ethnic elements that constituted early-nineteenth-century Mexico. Don Catrín repeatedly mixes different linguistic registers and styles, at times adopting a formal style in order to posture before his companions and at others reverting to a slangy, colloquial speech that breaks through his pretentious tone and calls attention to his shoddy education. He also has a penchant for brandishing poorly constructed and articulated Latin words and phrases in order to identify himself as a member of the educated elite, a tendency that generates highly amusing situations. Don Catrín's dodgy attempts to spout witticisms in Latin are translated for the reader in the footnotes.

Significantly, at a time when Spanish American writers tended to adhere to the rules and usages of Peninsular Spanish, Lizardi's language self-consciously mirrored the transformations that Spanish was undergoing as it adjusted to the Mexican context.[1] This feature contributed greatly to the popularity of Lizardi's works, for, as Jefferson Rea Spell notes, readers "recognized their legends, their superstitions, their manners and customs, and their speech in the story which he wove for them" ("Genesis" 58). Thus, while the slang, localisms, and colloquialisms in *Don Catrín* may present challenges to the translator and to the reader, they are essential elements that should find expression in the target text. One example of the novel's tendency to use such language appears in chapter 6, when Don Catrín uses the word *petate*, a term deriving from the Nahuatl word *pétatl*, a mat woven from palm leaves that served as the most common sleeping arrangement of the lower classes. While a case could be made in favor of translating the term simply as "mat" or "bed roll"—a decision that would arguably facilitate the reading process—this would deny readers the opportunity to appreciate the fusion of European and non-European cultures and languages from which Mexico was forged. Preserving Nahuatl-derived terms in the target text allows the reader to appreciate the presence of indigenous culture in colonial and postindependence Mexico as well as Lizardi's unique position within what would become a central debate in Latin America, the discourse on civilization versus barbarism.[2] At the time, many Spanish American intellectuals viewed indigenous, non-European peoples and cultural expressions as part of the supposed barbarism that stunted their nations' development. In *Don Catrín*, by contrast, it becomes clear that ignorance and bigotry are the obstacles on the path of Mexican progress, not the indigenous and mixed-race inhabitants that the narrator chauvenistically belittles.

Translators have emphasized the importance of making available to foreign audiences texts that question the notion of a homogenous national identity and culture in the source language. As Kathleen Ross has noted, this type of text helps undermine the "myths of national identity, built up over centuries, that present simplified and often homogenized versions of a country's inhabitants and customs" (136). For these reasons, I have put non-European and culture-specific terms in italics and provided explanatory footnotes for readers. For words that I determined could be translated with little detriment to the historical context, I have found rough equivalents in sources such as the *Diccionario de autoridades* (*Dictionary of Authority*).

While Lizardi's ability to represent the world he inhabited in a language that reflected the peculiarities of its people anticipated the arrival of Romanticism, Lizardi belongs more properly to the neoclassical movement.[3] Neoclassicism, with its emphasis on art's responsibility to the common good, was best suited to Lizardi's reformist project. In his works, Lizardi encouraged readers to improve themselves and their society through moral rectitude, education, and the exercise of reason. Another marked tendency of his novels is their adoption of elements of the picaresque, a literary mode with origins in sixteenth-century Spain and that some Spanish American writers still have recourse to today.[4] Picaresque works generally feature an antihero from the lower classes who, in his efforts to improve his station in society or simply to survive without doing any sort of work, tries his hand at various schemes, oftentimes sinking into delinquency. The fluid social movement of the *pícaro*, or rogue, permits an extensive representation of society and a bottom-up critique of its structures.[5] In *Don Catrín*, the narrator-protagonist's experience as a student, cadet, card sharp, beggar, and even a prisoner at the Morro Castle in Havana allows Lizardi to represent different social spaces and to identify numerous social ills for his reader. However, there are critical differences between the picaresque of Lizardi's novels, which some critics have described as "picaresca liberal" ("liberal picaresque"; Vela 98; my trans.), and works from the earlier Spanish tradition.[6] Unlike works such as *Lazarillo de Tormes* (1554), Lizardi's novels are critical without crossing into dark cynicism in their representations of society. Rather, his novels operate under a more optimistic view of man as a creature of reason capable of improvement through education. Significantly, in the novel, Don Catrín claims to have read Alain-René Lesage's *Gil Blas* (1715–35), a novel that was imitated by several subsequent writers and that mixes some of the techniques of the picaresque with neoclassical modes.

In addition to being a keen observer of his society, Lizardi was an avid reader who borrowed from multiple sources in the creation of his literary works. In fact, as Spell observes, Lizardi had a habit of keeping encyclopedias and other reference books at hand while he wrote ("Intellectual Background" 416). The titles of some of the sources used in Lizardi's *El Periquillo Sarniento* (*The Itching Parrot*) underscore the accessibility of Enlightenment texts in Mexico, which were oftentimes available in Spanish translation, and also provide a glimpse into Lizardi's literary and intellectual background. These sources include the following, among others: *Le grand dictionnaire historique, ou le mélange curieux de l'histoire sacrée et profane* (1674; *The Great Historical Dictionary; or, The Curious Mixture of Sacred and Profane History*), by the French scholar Louis Moréri; *De charlataneria eruditorum declamationes duae* (1715; *Declamations against the Charlatanry of the Learned*), by the German writer Johann Burckhard Mencke; *Riflessioni sopra il buon gusto intorno le scienze e le arti* (1708; *Reflections on Good Taste regarding the Sciences and Art*), by the Italian historian Ludovico Antonio Muratori; and *Pensées théologiques, relatives aux erreurs du temps* (1769; *Theological Thoughts on the Errors of the Times*), by the French ascetic writer Dom Nicolas Jamin. These texts provided rich sources for the ideas, maxims, and anecdotes presented in *El Periquillo Sarniento*.

While *El Periquillo*, the author's lengthy first novel, has been criticized for its long moralizing passages and extraneous anecdotes that distract from the main action, Lizardi exercised significant moderation in his use of outside textual material in *Don Catrín*.[7] The most frequent point of reference in *Don Catrín* is the Bible, from which the author selected stories and proverbs related to morality, work ethic, and even diet. The well-intentioned figures who try to steer Don Catrín to the straight and narrow all cite the Bible to underscore the error of his ways and his relentless desire "a subsistir con lujo y con regalo sin trabajar en nada, ni ser de modo alguno provechoso" ("to subsist with luxuries and comfort without doing any work or being useful in any way"; ch. 8). For example, toward the end of the novel when Don Catrín's health has deteriorated beyond any hope of recovery, Don Cándido turns to the proverbs of Solomon to prove that Don Catrín's maladies stem from years of poor diet and habits such as overeating, overdrinking, and oversleeping.

Another important source in *Don Catrín*, as well as in *El Periquillo Sarniento*, is *L'Ecole des moers* (1782; *The School of Manners*), by the French Jesuit priest and educator Jean-Baptiste Blanchard. From this text, which was available in Spanish translation, Lizardi culled the story about the seventeenth-century Swedish king who taught his soldiers a tough lesson about the ills of dueling (ch. 4). Blanchard's text also provided the comical story about how the French writer Chapelle, incensed by too much alcohol, tried to orchestrate a group suicide and how the French playwright Molière ingeniously tricked him out of it (ch. 13).[8] These anecdotes, which always deliver a clear lesson, are consistent with the moralizing impetus of the novel, and they allowed Lizardi to instruct his readers while at the same time entertaining them.

Lizardi points to other paratexts of possible significance in chapter 2 of the novel, when Don Catrín trumpets the works he has supposedly read. Don Catrín proclaims: "he leído una enciclopedia entera, el *Quijote* de Cervantes, el *Gil Blas*, las *Veladas de la quinta*, el *Viajero universal*, el *Teatro crítico*, el *Viaje al parnaso*, y un celemín de comedias y entremeses" ("I have read an encyclopedia from front to back, the *Quijote* by Cervantes, *Gil Blas*, *Soirees at the Chateau*, *The World Traveler*, *Critical Theater*, *Journey to Parnassus*, and bushels of comedies and intermezzos").[9] While one might expect Don Catrín to cite works of dubious value, this reading list, although relatively short, contains some texts that were foundational to Lizardi's own literary and intellectual formation. As mentioned, Lesage's *Gil Blas* provided a literary model for Lizardi's use of the picaresque. *Teatro crítico universal* (1726–39; *Universal Critical Theater*), for its part, was a principal work of the Spanish Enlightenment written by the Benedictine monk Benito Jerónimo Feijóo y Montenegro, many of whose ideas resonated deeply with Lizardi. Lizardi shared Feijóo y Montenegro's pedagogical zeal as well as his critical attitude toward inherited nobility and his belief in the need for men to assume useful trades. Another important reference is to Miguel de Cervantes, who wrote *Don Quijote* (1605, 1615) and *Viaje del Parnaso* (1614; *Journey of Parnassus*) and whose influence on Lizardi has been widely studied. Like some of his fellow Spanish American writers, Lizardi continued to be an impassioned reader of Spanish golden age and baroque literature, even as he adopted tenets of neoclassicism. For its part, *Veillees du château* (1784; *Soirees at the Chateau*), by Stéphanie-Félicité du Crest de Genlis, is a collection of fables meant for the improvement of young women. Lizardi was very concerned with women's roles in society, especially with regard to motherhood, and he examined these carefully in his novel *La Quijotita y su prima* (1819; *Little Miss Quixote and Her Cousin*).

In order to situate the text within the time period when Lizardi put pen to paper, I have strived to adopt language that would be perceived by readers as contemporary with the source text, and I have tried to avoid markedly modern words and expressions.[10] Part of my strategy consisted in multiple, meticulous readings of the source text, during which time I mulled over linguistic options that would best convey the meaning, style, and tone of the different speakers while adhering to linguistic tendencies of nineteenth-century English. To paraphrase Gregory Rabassa, I tried to imagine what the voices in the novel would have sounded like had their native tongue been English (121). Where I lacked adequate words and expressions, I turned to eighteenth- and nineteenty-century texts, with an eye to picaresque works such as Henry Fielding's *Tom Jones* (1749), William Makepeace Thackeray's *The Luck of Barry Lyndon* (1844), and on the American side, Hugh Henry Brackenridge's *Modern Chivalry* (1815). These texts were especially helpful when it came to finding natural-sounding slang and playful euphemisms characteristic of nineteenth-century English.

Explanations are offered for some of the important locations mentioned in Lizardi's novel. The narrator-protagonist refers to theaters, prisons, plazas, convents, and more as he makes his way around the city. These references are rife with cultural significance and constitute vital elements of Lizardi's portrait of the Mexico of his time. To familiarize readers with these spaces, I drew on Luis González Obregón's *Época colonial* (*Colonial Era*) and Enrique de Olvarría y Ferrari's *Teatro en México* (*Theater in Mexico*). In this way, readers of the translation will learn about the Parián, a bustling market in Mexico City that was demolished during the government of Santa Anna; a theater called the *Coliseo*, or Coliseum, which was located inside a hospital for impoverished Indians; city plazas; and other important landmarks, many of which exist only in Mexico's past.

Lizardi's original notes to the text, which I have translated here into English, are indicated with asterisks. (Where two notes belonging to Lizardi appear on the same page, the first is indicated with an asterisk, the second with a dagger.) Notes belonging to the editor and translator are numbered.

Notes

1. Indicative of Lizardi's interest in recording Mexican Spanish is the glossary of terms that he wrote to accompany his first and much longer novel, *El Periquillo Sarniento* (1816–31; *The Itching Parrot*).

2. The discourse of civilization versus barbarism was articulated powerfully by the Argentine writer and politician Domingo Faustino Sarmiento. In his influential text *Facundo* (1845), Sarmiento described Argentina as a space divided by two antithetical societies: "la una española, europea, civilizada, y la otra bárbara, americana, casi indígena" ("the one Spanish, European, civilized, the other barbaric, American, almost indigenous"; 33; my trans.).

3. Spanish American writers of the time had access to works by important figures of the Spanish Enlightenment, such as Benito Jerónimo Feijóo y Montenegro, Gregorio Mayans y Siscar, and Andrés Piquer y Arrufat, and became familiar with French neoclassical and classical writers through translations. One important text, Nicolas Boileau's *L'Art poétique* (1674; *The Art of Poetry*), which set forth the ideals of truth, wit, and imitation of nature, was available in a Spanish translation by Ignacio de Luzán (Monguió 104).

4. As a reader of this translation has pointed out, the Mexican writer Homer Aridjis made use of the picaresque mode in his novel *Juan Cabezón* (1985).

5. For more on Lizardi's use of the picaresque in *El Periquillo Sarniento*, see Salomon; see also Franco 34.

6. In *Fundamentos de la literatura mexicana* (*Foundations of Mexican Literature*), Arqueles Vela categorizes the picaresque of *El Periquillo Sarniento* and *Don Catrín* as "picaresca liberal" ("liberal picaresque"; 98; my trans.), contrasting it with that of works like Miguel Alemán's *Guzmán de Alfarache* (1599), which Vela designates "picaresca del absolutismo" ("picaresque of absolutism"; 98; my trans.). For more on Lizardi's adoption and adaptation of the picaresque, see Borgeson.

7. Spell examines some of the texts that informed Lizardi's thinking and influenced his literary production; see "Educational Views" and "Intellectual Background."

8. Chapelle likely refers to the French writer and dramatist Jean de La Chapelle.

9. The title of Cervantes's text is actually *Viaje del Parnaso* (*Journey of Parnassus*), not *Viaje al Parnaso* (*Journey to Parnassus*).

10. This translation's style may be described as falling somewhere between "time-matched archaisation" and "updated archaisation," as defined by Jones and Turner.

Works Cited

Borgeson, Paul W. "Problemas de técnica narrativa en dos novellas de Lizardi." *Hispania*, vol. 69, no. 3, 1986, pp. 504–11.

Diccionario de autoridades. Facsimile reprint of the 1726–37 ed., Editorial Gredos, 1963.

Franco, Jean. *An Introduction to Spanish-American Literature*. Cambridge UP, 1969.

González Obregón, Luis. *Época colonial: México viejo, noticias históricas, tradiciones, leyendas y costumbres*. Librería Viuda de C. Bouret, 1900.

Jones, F. Robertson, and Alexander W. Turner. "Archaisation, Modernisation and Reference in the Translation of Older Texts." *Across Languages and Cultures*, vol. 5, no. 2, 2004, pp. 159–85.

Monguió, Luis. "La poética neoclásica en la América Hispana." *Revista de Crítica Literaria Latinoamericana*, nos. 43–44, 1996, pp. 103–17.

Olvarría y Ferrari, Enrique de. *Teatro en México*. 2nd ed., vol. 1, La Europea, 1895.

Rabassa, Gregory. *If This Be Treason: Translation and Its Dyscontents: A Memoir*. New Directions Books, 2005.

Ross, Kathleen. "Identity and Relationships in the Context of Latin America." *Literature in Translation: Teaching Issues and Reading Practices*, edited by Carol Maier and Françoise Massardier-Kenney, Kent State UP, 2010, pp. 136–47.

Salomon, Noël. "La crítica del sistema colonial de la Nueva España en *El Periquillo Sarniento*." *Cuadernos Americanos*, vol. 21, no. 138, 1965, pp. 167–79.

Sarmiento, Domingo Faustino. *Facundo: Civilización y barbarie: Vida de Juan Facundo Quiroga*. Introduction by Raimundo Lazo, 10th ed., Porrúa, 1998.

Spell, Jefferson Rea. "The Educational Views of Fernández de Lizardi." *Hispania*, vol. 9, no. 5, 1926, pp. 259–74.

———. "The Genesis of the First Mexican Novel." *Hispania*, vol. 14, no. 1, 1931, pp. 53–58.

———. "The Intellectual Background of Lizardi as Reflected in *El Periquillo Sarniento*." *PMLA*, vol. 71, no. 3, 1956, pp. 414–32.

Vela, Arqueles. *Fundamentos de la literatura mexicana*. Patria, 1953.

JOSÉ JOAQUÍN FERNÁNDEZ DE LIZARDI

Life and Deeds of the Famous Gentleman
Don Catrín de la Fachenda

Contents

CHAPTER 1

IN WHICH HE GIVES A JUSTIFICATION FOR HIS WORK AND AN ACCOUNT OF HIS HOMELAND, PARENTS, BIRTH, AND UPBRINGING

I would be a most indolent man, deserving of the scourges of the universe, if I deprived my companions and friends of this precious little book in whose composition I have racked my brains, exhausting my not unexceptional talents, my vast erudition, and my sublime and sententious style.

No, no longer shall my companion and friend the *Periquillo Sarniento*[1] boast that his work found such a warm reception in this province, for mine, disburdened of inopportune episodes, fastidious digressions, tedious moralisms, and reduced to a single tome as an octavo book, will naturally be more appreciated and more legible: not only will it wander from hand to hand, satchel to satchel, and pillow to pillow, but from city to city, kingdom to kingdom, nation to nation, and it will not stop until

---

[1] The narrator refers to the title and protagonist of Lizardi's much longer novel of 1816, *El Periquillo Sarniento* (*The Itching Parrot*).

thousands upon thousands of printings have been made at each of the four corners of the earth.

Yes, my fellow Catrines[2] and companions, this famous work will run . . . nay, I spoke wrong, it will fly on the wings of fame throughout every part of the inhabited and even uninhabited world; it will be printed in Spanish, English, French, German, Italian, Arabic, Tatar, etc., and every last son of Adam, without a single exception, upon hearing the sonorous and pleasant name of Don[3] Catrín, its one and only, most erudite author, will bow his head and confess its commendable merit.

And how could it be but so, when the objective that I propose is among the most interesting and the method among the most solid and effective? The objective is to increase the number of Catrines; the method, to propose my life as a model for all . . . Here, in short, is all that the reader should desire to know about my intentions in writing the story of my life—but what life? That of

---

[2] Plural of *catrín*, an individual who attempts to imitate members of the upper socioeconomic classes by manipulating his public appearance and behavior. Like the British version, the fop or dandy, the *catrín* is generally characterized as ostentatious, devoted to fashion, and concerned about his appearance (see introduction). I have chosen to capitalize the term in the novel, as the narrator adopts it to describe the family to which he belongs.

[3] In Spanish, *don* is an honorific title that precedes the first name. Originally, it was reserved for certain people of high social status.

a gentleman illustrious by birth, most wise by his studies, opulent in riches, exemplary in conduct, and a hero through and through. But enough of this preamble, *operibus credite.*[4] Observe closely.

I was born, for your honor and example, in this opulent and densely populated city in the year 1790 or 1791. Thus, I am thirty or thirty-one years old at the moment that I write my story, in the flower of youth, an age when one should not expect to find such mature literary and moral fruits the likes of which you will all see in the course of this little book. But just as each century is wont to produce a hero, it came down to me to become the wonder of the eighteenth century, in which I was born, like I said, to parents as illustrious as Caesar, as good and agreeable as I could have ever wished them to be, and such consummate Catrines, whose lineage I am in no way undeserving.

My parents, then, clean of any inferior race[5] as well as of any wealth—inclination of all men of merit!—

---

[4] . . . *et non verbis* ("Believe in works and not words"), an allusion to John 10.38: "even though you do not believe me, believe the miracles" (*Bible*). All subsequent citations of the Bible are taken from this edition.

[5] Lizardi makes strategic use of his narrator to undermine notions of racial purity and impurity. Don Catrín is an antihero who embodies many of society's ills, and his disparagement of indigenous people, peasants, and people of mixed race serves as a critique of the bigotry of the time.

raised me as they themselves were raised, and I came out equally advantaged.

Although I say that my parents were poor, I do not mean they were destitute. My mother brought to my father a dowry of two boys and three thousand pesos.[6] The two boys were the unacknowledged fruits of a nobleman, as were the three thousand pesos, children of his as well, which he gave to her for the boys' maintenance. My father understood everything; but how could he not dissemble for two boys gilded with three thousand shekels from the Indies? Thus, I reveal to you the illustriousness of my birth, the merit of my mother, and the unquestionable honor of my father. But I do not want to boast of these things; the lush family trees that adorn my letters patent of nobility and the positions that my worthy ancestors held in the splendid professions of arms and letters will shelter me *usque in aeternum*[7] from charges of braggart and prevaricator, when I assure you on my honor as Don Catrín that I am noble, illustrious, and distinguished by act, by fact, and by stature.

---

[6] As David L. Frye explains, the peso was the basic coin of colonial Mexico: "The peso was divided into eight *reales*—sometimes divided literally, by snapping a peso into eight bits, though the *real* . . . was also produced as a silver coin in its own right" (xxxix).

[7] "Forever."

But, returning to the subject of my story, I proclaim that by blind fortune I was born, at least, with enough respectability and means to ensure that my upbringing would be brilliant.

Of treasures my parents had none but those coins necessary to raise me, which they did with the greatest pampering. Nothing that I wanted was denied me, everything about me was praised, even if I upset or disturbed guests. At the age of twelve, the servants waited on me hand and foot, and my parents had to beseech me not to reproach them angrily—such was their virtue, such their prudence, and so great was their love for me!

To appease an uncle in the priesthood, eternal pest and my declared enemy *ab ineunte aetate*,[8] or from my first years, they put me in school, or, more precisely, in schools, for I attended at least fourteen. This is because at some I hit boys over the head and at others I squared off with the teacher; at some I romped around all day and at others I played truant four or five times a week. At one I learned to read Christian doctrine according to the catechism of Ripalda,[9] to count a little, and to write badly, for I considered myself a rich boy, and my friends

---

[8] "From the earliest infancy."
[9] By the Spanish Jesuit Fray Jerónimo de Martínez de Ripalda (1536–1618).

9

the Catrines told me that it was very improper for nobles as well brought up as I to have elegant penmanship or to know the vulgar symbols of the useless alphabet. I did not need much encouraging to flee from the bothersome guidance of those nuisances who call themselves sensible; and so I made sure to read and count badly, and to write worse.

What does it matter to me, my beloved Catrines, relatives, friends, and companions, I repeat, what does it matter to me if I read this way or that, if I say twenty plus eleven is thirty-six, or if I write *the priest of Tacubaya went out to prey on the mountain?*[10] They tell me this is nonsense, that priests do not *prey* on mountains but rather *pray* on mountains, that *prey* with an *e* in our language means to hunt or catch an animal for food while *pray* with an *a* is to implore or give thanks to God. I ask you again, what do these importunate reproaches matter to me? Nothing, in truth, nothing at all, because I have met many rich people who wrote like dogs; and they were flattered and commended as the most capable scribes in the universe, all of which makes me believe, dear ones, that all merit and cleverness consists in know-

---

[10] In the Spanish text, Don Catrín does not confuse the words *pray* and *prey* but rather the words *cazar* ("to hunt") and *casar* ("to wed"), which sound similar.

ing how to acquire and preserve the fruits of the American hills.[11]

As I was telling you, I turned out to be a very talented student, and my parents put me in college so that I would study, for these good folks said that a Don Catrín must never learn a trade, for that would be to degrade himself, but that in any case I should study so that one day I would be minister of state or at the very least a man of great influence in the Indies.

I was at that time humbler or had less understanding of my own merit, and therefore I did not think about honors or ostentation but about playing all day, having fun, and living pleasurably.

The impertinent teachers used to scold me and oblige me to study now and then, and at those times . . . oh, to behold such colossal talent!, at those few times that I studied by force, I learned Nebrija's *Gramática*[12] and all of

---

[11] While a reader in the United States might interpret the term *American* to refer to the United States, in Spanish the term *América* and its adjective forms are commonly used to refer to the continents of North and South America collectively.

[12] Antonio de Nebrija (1441–1522) was a Spanish humanist and scholar of language who wrote important works about classical Latin as well as Spanish. Recognizing the vital role that language played in the governance of the state, he codified for the first time the Spanish vernacular language in his renowned *Gramática de la lengua castellana* (1492; *Grammar of the Castilian Language*).

Cicero's[13] Latin in a twinkling, but with such felicity that I was the joy of my fellow students and the envy of my tedious teachers. The former would laugh as I translated a verse of Virgil or Horace, and the latter would become green with envy upon hearing me make an example of a Latin phrase, because at every turn I made them see the limits of their own talents and the breadth of mine.

They would tell me, for example, that *ego, mei* does not have a vocative, and I would tell them that it is easy and necessary to give it one, for without the vocative, one could not write the following oration in Latin: *Woe is me, the most unfortunate of all who are born!*, and by adding the vocative *ego*, we can say: *O ego infelicior natorum*, and thus, the difficulty is solved, and one can overcome other such stinginess and injustices of the ancient grammarians in the same way.[14]

---

[13] Marcus Tullius Cicero (106–43 BCE) was a Roman lawyer, orator, and statesman who transformed the Latin language. He is also remembered for defending Republican principles during Julius Caesar's rise to power. The four separate references to Cicero in the novel may be attributed, on the one hand, to Lizardi's interest in the persuasive power of language, and on the other, to the fact that the Roman orator was admired by Enlightenment thinkers, whose work in turn influenced Lizardi's reformist project (Gay 260–61).

[14] Don Catrín is making a bad joke, suggesting that the "I" in Latin can be in both the nominative case and the vocative case—that is, that "I" can be both the subject and the addressee of the sentence. This scene pokes fun at the Latin language, wherein it is difficult for a person to address themself if grammatical rules are to be followed strictly. More broadly, the scene criticizes traditional educa-

The resistance that I gave to all grammar was most lucid; there was not one who did not erupt in laughter upon hearing me translate that worn-out verse of Virgil:

Tityre, tu patulae recubans sub tegmine fagi,[15] which I translated in this way: *tu recubans,* you will cover; *Tityre,* the Titans; *patulae,* of the patchouli; *fagi,* with a fig; *sub tegmine,* under certain terms. All would laugh, celebrating, naturally, my ability, but the teachers would get red in the face, looking as if they wanted to throttle me from their seats, such was the envy that afflicted them! But, in short, I received my regalia, my parents were contented, and they arranged for me to study philosophy.

I proved as proficient in this field as I did in grammar. Within two months I was arguing in syllogisms so well that it was astonishing, and I had an *ergo* so thunderous that it shook the robust columns of the school, always to the amazement of my fellow students and to the great envy of my teachers.

<hr />

tion in Mexico at the time and its emphasis on established norms, dogma, Aristotelian logic, and hidebound rules. For more on Lizardi's ideas regarding education and on the thinkers who influenced him, see Spell.

[15] From Virgil's *First Eclogue*: "You, Tityrus, lying under the shade of a spreading beech" (my trans.). Don Catrín bases his translation of Latin into Spanish on phonetic similarities, producing a fumbling version of Virgil's classic text.

On one occasion, arguing with a stale Peripatetic[16] who defended the existence of a certain animal referred to as "reasoning being" by its long-established defenders, after several things that I said to him, I added this forceful syllogism:

Si per alicujus actus efficeretur entis ratio, maxime per huic: per huic non; ergo per nullius.[17] The tables and benches of the classroom resonated with the palm-slapping of the students, whose raucous laughter prevented the argument from continuing; the Peripatetic gave me a firm hug and a half *real*[18] with a likeness depicted on it, saying to me:

"I will have you know, it is easier to create a reasoning being than to devise another syllogism in such elaborate and elegant Latin."

Everyone applauded me, everyone celebrated me that day, and someone even wrote the syllogism in gold letters and put it above the doors of the classroom with this motto: *Ad perpetuam rei memoriam, et ad nostri Catrinis gloriam*, which translated meant:[19] "To the glory of the

---

[16] A follower of the philosophical school of Aristotle.

[17] This sentence is nonsense that only sounds like Latin, and it highlights the character's ignorance.

[18] The *real* was a coin used in colonial Mexico that was worth eight pesos (Frye xxxix).

[19] At certain moments in the source text, such as this one, Don Catrín specifies that he is translating Latin into *castellano*, or Castilian,

14

memory of the Latinary history of the illustrious Ca-trín, who is one of our Catrines."[20] What do you think, friends and companions? Are you not amazed by such talent in so few years? Are you not astonished by my fame at such an early age? Is my conduct not an example for you all? Well, imitate me and you will achieve such accolades.

Two and a half years of courses in the arts passed, during which I had the great honor of completing university and secondary school with full honors from my professors and fellow collegians.

At the end of this time, as the reward seemed insignificant, I refused to obtain the highest honors *in rectum*[21] that they offered me and contented myself with the title of bachelor, which cost my father thirty-some pesos, I believe. I consented to this because I knew how necessary it is to have a bachelor of arts to acquire the degree of graduate, doctor, or teacher; and as the bachelor of arts is *conditio sine qua non*,[22] it was necessary for me to complete my studies despite my disinclination.

---

a synonym for the Spanish language. Preserving these references to Spanish in an English translation would be incongruous, so I have removed them.

[20] A more accurate translation of this motto would be the following: "To the everlasting memory of the deeds and the glory of our beloved Catrín."

[21] "Directly."

[22] "A necessary, indispensable condition."

Nevertheless, with my great title and eighteen years upon my shoulders, I had fun on my vacations, passing the time with my companions and friends, who were many, and as instructed and as good as I.

Well, my uncle the priest thought I was wasting time, and he pressed my parents to bury me once again in college to pursue advanced studies, instructing them, however, to consult my opinion in order to proceed correctly.

I had no desire to continue a career as cumbersome as that of letters, for two very powerful reasons: first, to avoid suffering the envy of my teachers when they saw how my talents overshadowed theirs; and second, because I considered myself so enlightened with the studying that I had already done, that I could dispute any branch of knowledge with Solomon himself.

Thus determined, I told my father that I did not want to continue my studies, because the fields of inquiry were nothing more than bothersome charlatanry whose only rewards were afflictions of the spirit and headaches; for every half-wit who reaps the fruits of his literary efforts, nine hundred are forgotten and end their days in neglect and penury.

My father had talent, but as he recognized the many advantages of mine, he shrugged his shoulders as if he were surprised and did nothing more than relay this message to my tedious uncle the priest, who, because of this, delivered a bothersome speech to me, as you will see in the chapter that follows.

Chapter 2

In which is described the figure of his uncle the priest, what he discussed with Catrín and his friend Precioso, and the results

How true it is that, were it not for meddlers in our families, everything would move along with greater order! More often than not, however, these prudent advisers bring discord into our homes.

My good uncle was the priest of Jalatlaco, of which you have all heard mention in this kingdom. He troubled himself over that which did not concern him, and the most distant of predicaments left him looking worn out and gaunt; how must it be, then, when he judged that the problem lay with one of his kin? God of my soul! Then everything was consternation, fear, and affliction; there was no advice he would not give, no act he would not perform, to prevent the misfortune that lay in wait. Sometimes he got his way by force of reprimands and sermons; but at others, which were the greater part, he preached his sermon in the desert,[23] and everything remained as it was.

That is how it happened with me one day . . . but first I will sketch his figure for you all, so that you can understand how different his thoughts were from mine; for if one knows the tree by its fruit, one usually knows a man's character by his exterior.[24]

My good uncle was, as I was saying, an old priest of about sixty years, tall, gaunt, ashen, with a venerable face and a serious, even-tempered gaze. The years had whitened his locks, and his studies and illnesses, devouring his health, had divested his gums of teeth, lined the skin of his face with wrinkles, and clouded the vision of his blue eyes, which took refuge beneath handsome lashes and a large brow. However, in his prominent forehead one could read the serenity of a good conscience—that is, if good consciences are painted upon wide foreheads and colossal bald spots. His discourses were well-composed, and the words he used to deliver them were sweet, and sometimes, or rather always when it concerned me, harsh. His dress was always fashioned according to the modesty and humility inherent in his character. His

---

[23] Matthew 3.1: "In those days John the Baptist came, preaching in the Desert of Judea."
[24] Matthew 7.16: "By their fruit you will recognize them."

hands along with his heart were open to the destitute, and all that he earned through the priesthood he invested in the aid of his poor parishioners, and in this way he was naturally liked by all who knew him, save for me, who, truth be told, could not stomach him, for, being my uncle and being that he loved me dearly, he was my undying pedagogue, my watchful prosecutor, and my perpetual castigator.

Had it not been for my loving parents—perish the thought!—the priest would have certainly transformed me into a hateful misanthrope or into an anchorite; but my parents, may holy glory keep them, loved me more than the priest did, and they used to liberate me from his impertinence. A *no* from my lips, spoken with resolution to my mother, was worth more than twenty of my uncle's sermons; as soon as they saw me unhappy, they would indulge my will and try to pacify me. Such is to know what it means to fulfill one's obligations as family men and women; such is how children are raised and how they grow up fit to honor their parents' memory eternally.

One day, as I was saying, my unendurable uncle called me aside and said to me:

"Catrín, why don't you want to continue your studies? For good or bad, you have already begun your degree in the arts; nobody is crowned nor earns his laurels without making it to the end. It is true that studying is cumbersome at first; but a fact no less true is that its fruits are sweet and invariably yield results. So then, why don't you want to continue?"

"Sir," I answered him, "because I am convinced of the uselessness of the fields of study, of the meagerness of the fruits reaped by the wise, and because I already know enough from my studies and the sundry reading to which I have dedicated myself."

"What is that you say?" said the priest. "Explain yourself, what sort of sundry reading was it? Because if it resembles your ponderous studies, it is useless."

"Nothing less than this," I responded: "I have read an encyclopedia from front to back, the *Quijote* by Cervantes, *Gil Blas, Soirees at the Chateau, The World Traveler, Critical Theater, Journey to Parnassus*, and bushels of comedies and intermezzos."[25]

"Well, after your readings you consider yourself a bona fide wise man; but understand, to your confusion, that you are nothing more than a swollen-headed fool. By way of your idiocies, you will increase the number

---

[25] Readers might expect Don Catrín to cite works of questionable value, but this reading list contains certain texts that were important to Lizardi's own literary and intellectual development. For more, see this volume's Note on the Translation.

of men masquerading as sages and scholars *a la violeta*.[26] What is this about the sciences being useless? What can you tell me about this that I do not already know? You will tell me, yes, that knowledge is very difficult to acquire even after prolonged study, because a man's whole life, even if he lives to be more than one hundred, is not long enough to understand a single field of inquiry in all its depth. God alone is the knower of all things and the being from whom nothing is hidden; but imperfect and mortal man hardly manages, at the end of a thousand pains, to know a jot more than the rest of his fellow men. Hence, I will agree with you in acknowledging that there is not, nor has there been, nor will there be on the face of the earth a single man completely knowledgeable in theology, jurisprudence, medicine, chemistry, astronomy, or in any other discipline that we know and understand; but this only proves that, in spite of everything he might do, man is limited—not that it is impossible to climb and reach the summit of knowledge, and much less that these are useless.

"What would you say if you knew that toward the middle of the last century the Genevan philosopher, the great Jean-Jacques Rousseau, wrote a discourse proving

---

[26] *Eruditos a la violeta* (1772; *Would-Be Scholars*), by the Spanish writer José de Cadalso y Vázquez, presents a critique of false erudition and of those who pretend to be cultivated.

21

that the fields of inquiry were at odds with the practice of virtue and that they engendered an inclination toward vice in their professors, and that this discourse was awarded by the Academy of Dijon in France?[27] You, who are so poorly educated, would have thought you had stopped the sun in its course; but no, my son. This great man abused his talent in order to prove a ridiculous paradox. In his discourse, he set out to prove that the arts and the sciences were pernicious after having professed their advantages, savored them, and having managed just as surely to immortalize his name through them. Such is the vanity of man. With his eloquence, Rousseau defended a delirium that he himself condemned in his heart, and his eloquence was so great that it deluded scholars from a respected academy, so much that they awarded a prize for what merited scorn. But this proves that the usefulness of the fields of study can go a long way, for if the art of speech makes praiseworthy that which is foolish, what could it do if it were applied to that which is useful and advantageous?

"You will also tell me, as you have told me already, that the wise man's lot is a wretched one, and that for

---

[27] *Discours sur les sciences et les arts* (1750; *Discourse on the Sciences and the Arts*); notwithstanding the priest's scathing rant about the discourse, Lizardi agreed with many of the Genevan philosopher's ideas, especially where these pertained to education.

every wise man that the world celebrates, a thousand are pummeled to the ground and persecuted. However, knowledge is not to blame for this, but rather the disorder of ideas and other things that you would not understand even if I explained them to you. However, in spite of all this, the wise man never fails to perceive the fruit of his labors within himself. The ignorant man, although he may be rich, cannot use his gold to buy the pleasures that the wise man enjoys even in the midst of his misfortune. The former has flatterers who will try to extract from him something hidden. The latter has people who appreciate him, love him, and praise him for his merit and his merit alone. Ultimately, the fool will call himself fortunate as long as he is rich; the wise man, if he unites enlightenment with virtue, will be truly fortunate even in adversity. In the light of this, Cicero wisely said: 'all life's pleasures change with time, age, and location; but one's education gives nourishment to youth and happiness to old age, delivers brilliance in prosperity, and serves as an asset and a comfort in adversity.' Hence, you should surmise that the branches of knowledge are never useless, that the wise always perceive the fruit of their labors, and that if you want to achieve anything, it is necessary to continue what you started. This I tell you for your own good; do what you like, for you are grown now."

Saying this, the good priest left without waiting for a response, leaving me much chafed by his impertinent sermon.

To put this unpleasant episode behind me, I took my cape and went to tell my troubles to a close friend named Precioso, a youth who was not only cultivated but refined and polite to the extreme, of astonishing erudition, exemplary manners, and perfectly suited to me.

When I arrived at his house, he was sitting before his dressing table applying color to his cheeks with I know not what concoction. Upon seeing me, he paid me all the necessary compliments and asked me the reason for my visit. I told him all that had passed, adding:

"So you see, my friend, a degree in the arts is long, onerous, and not at all dependable in this kingdom. Say I consider taking a position as an apprentice in an office; after five or six years of laboring for free, when a vacancy opens in a position that I deserve, some so-and-so will show up decked out in recommendations. They'll pick him over me and I'll be out on the street. If it's not that, then it will be my handwriting, which is so poor that they would have to be pharmacists to understand it, which is a good reason not to want to be an office worker. If I chanced upon a position in business that could afford me a comfortable life, I would reject it because it would be beneath the nobility of my lineage, for, as you know, a Don Catrín doesn't aspire to be a ragpicker, and much less to plunk himself down in a tavern or behind an oil-and-vinegar counter. The idea of becoming the administrator of some country farm is ridiculous, for, besides the fact that I have no training in it, the position of laborer is for the Indians, peasants, and other such lowly people.[28] And so you see, I don't know what profession I can take up that will provide me money, honor, and little work."

"Why, you couldn't fight your way out of a paper bag," Precioso answered. "Is there anything easier than being a soldier? Why don't you consider it? The profession could not be more highly regarded; you work little and loaf a lot, and the king always pays according to the rank you obtain."

"It's true," I said, "your proposal appeals to me; but there's a considerable snag in that plan, which is, namely, that . . . well, I'm not a coward, but I'm not used to battles nor brawls, and I can't imagine myself facing off with the enemy on the battleground. No, I'm incapable of shedding the blood of my fellow man, much less of risking that my own be shed; I'm very sensitive."

---

[28] Throughout the novel, Lizardi uses his narrator to faithfully represent, and criticize, the bigotry of the time.

"I understand you," Precioso responded. "You may be very sensitive or just very chickenhearted, but I guarantee that as soon as you get through the first few skirmishes you'll lose your fear and sensitivity in no time; it's just a matter of doing it. So come on, ask your father to dress you in the braided cords of my regiment, and you'll see what a sweet life we'll make for ourselves."

My friends' wholesome doctrines held great authority over my heart back then. I adopted Precioso's outlook straightaway and returned mad with joy to my house, determined to be a cadet at all costs.

It did not take me a lot of work, for while my father resisted at first, alleging that he was penniless at the moment and that he could not provide me with the refinements expected of the distinguished cadet class, in the end I pressed, importuned, and fought with my mother, who, in order not to see me angry, said that she would convince my father even if it left them without a mattress.

These promises were not in vain, for my mother did so much that, by the next day, my father had changed his mind and asked me what regiment I wanted to join as a cadet, and learning that it was the very same one as Precioso's, he assured me that in a week's time I would be wearing braided military cords. And that is just what happened, as I will tell you in a separate chapter.

Chapter 3

Which relates how he became a
cadet, the warnings of his uncle the
priest, and Tremendo's campaign

Nothing is out of reach when one has coins and one's nobility, and my experience made this clear to me. My father prepared his request on my behalf, presenting the letters patent verifying that I was a *hidalgo*[29] and confirming the commendable merit of my grandparents, who had been conquistadors,[30] and in the blink of an eye I had the licenses necessary to join the armed forces.

As predicted, my famous uniform was ready within four days, and I put it on the following Sunday, to my own great joy and to that of my parents, friends, and all my relatives, save for the priest, who, accustomed to dealing with the peasants from his parish, was entirely opposed to the opulence of the court and the lavishness of its gentlemen; as such, he was very opposed to my new employment. And that was not the worst of it, for he tried to talk my father out of it until the last day. But

---

[29] In Spain, a person who belonged to the lower nobility.

[30] Spanish and Portuguese soldiers and explorers who, beginning at the turn of the sixteenth century, came to the Americas to claim territory in the name of their respective empires.

he did not succeed: I donned the braided cords and that night there was a magnificent ball at our house.

Everyone embraced me and congratulated me ceaselessly, and between the toasts that were made to my health, the guests told me I looked like a captain general, and in this fashion they helped me better understand my merit.

Only the priest, God forgive the blessed priest, was my constant torment. When the event ended, he said to me:

"I am your uncle; I love you sincerely. I desire your success and well-being, and you are entering a profession where these can only be attained by men of disciplined conduct, and I fear greatly that it is not a desire to serve the king and your homeland that has led you to this point, but rather a love of libertinage. If this is so, know that just as there are unscrupulous soldiers, there are also respected officers who make them carry out their duties or expel them disgracefully in serious cases. If you turn out to be as bad a soldier as you were a student, you will reap equal applause, praise, and admiration. And finally, know that even if you succeed in being tolerated as a libertine, at the hour of your death you will find a supreme and inexorable judge who will punish your crimes with an eternity of sorrows. May God help you and good night."

This was the congratulations that the priest gave me, and I was left as grateful as I could be under the circumstances, for his last threat left me disconcerted. However, the next day I went to search for my friends, whom I found in a café, and as soon as they saw me they implored me to drink *aguardiente*,[31] a request that I was happy to satisfy.

As toasts were made to our health, there was no woman in Mexico whose honor wasn't used as a rag to wipe our mouths, and not a single reputation escaped unstained. Among my chums, there was Don Taravilla,[32] a twenty-year-old youth, an unrivaled talker, and a Catrín through and through—that is, a man of propriety and of very attractive circumstances. He would liven up a *tertulia*[33] single-handedly; no one uttered a word when he began to speak, and although he had a tendency to

---

[31] *Aguardiente*, a compound of the Spanish words *agua* ("water") and *ardiente* ("burning"), is an alcoholic beverage that can be made at home by distilling substances such as sugarcane, grain, tubers, and different types of fruit.

[32] A variation of the spelling of the Spanish word *tarabilla*, which means "chatterbox."

[33] A social gathering that normally takes place in a café and in which discussions often center on literature or politics. The tradition has its roots in Spain, and it is still practiced in Spain and parts of Spanish America. A *tertulia* is also a place designated for playing billiards, cards, or dominoes.

discredit others, no one bothered to do anything, on account of the great wit and generality with which he would do it.

On this occasion, I recall that he declared that none among us could swear to be the son of his father, and he added:

"For my part, at any rate, I'll never profess to believe nor guarantee such a thing. My mother is young and beautiful, her husband is old and poor; it's for all of you to say if I can swear that he's my father. But what does it matter to me? He provides for me, my mother is a woman, and I must forgive her weaknesses."

How would a man who speaks this way about himself speak of others? In less than half an hour he shredded the honor of ten well-known maidens, shattered the good name of six wives, brought the reputation of twenty businessmen tumbling to the ground, and defamed four serious men of the church, prelates no less. And if the conversation had lasted longer, the robe, the church's stipends, and the staff and crosier of Mexico[34] would have been reduced to dust on his lips. Such was his volubility! Such was his grace!

---

[34] Don Catrín refers metonymically to figures of authority in Mexico. By the image of the robe, he refers to judges; by the church's stipends, to priests; by the staff, to law officers; and by the crosier, to bishops.

I could not help but recall what my uncle the priest had told me the previous night; and so, feeling confused, and propping myself up at the table with my hand on my forehead and the bottle in front of me, I thought to myself:

"There is nothing to be done. This sort of banter, in which no reputation is safe, surely cannot please God or be advantageous to men. To speak and listen to such cruel charges can be nothing less than wrong, for they injure one's fellow man, and this is at odds with charity, and our religion assures us that he who does not love his fellow man as he loves himself disobeys the law, and he who disobeys the law sins, and he who sins with delight, knowingly and repeatedly, dissents, and he who dissents lives badly, and he who lives badly almost always dies badly, and he who dies badly condemns himself, and he who condemns himself will suffer without end. My God! This is what the priest was trying to tell me last night!"

So intoxicated was I by these gloomy considerations that I wasn't even paying attention to what my friends were saying. My introspection was so noticeable that a certain Don—how should I know what his name was? They called him Don Tremendo, an officer from the regiment N—took note of it and rebuked me for it. I told him about what had befallen me the night before with my uncle, and that the fear his speech had instilled in me was the cause of my consternation.

A choir of mockery was the response that my confession received; everyone roared with laughter, and this fellow Tremendo managed to amplify everyone's elation, saying:

"A valiant one have we for a companion in arms! You poor devil, why didn't you try for the Capuchin's veil[35] instead of the cadet's braided cords, or at least the spit in the kitchen of a convent of friars, since you're so faint-hearted and scrupulous? Here, here! It looks like we have ourselves a proper coward. Look at yourself, here you are, a not-so-ugly boy with four coins in your pocket and some cords draped over your shoulder, and you're frightened by two tales that your uncle told you . . . Well, your uncle, that old creeping Jesus, that utter fanatic and fool whom I would have told to go to hell a long time ago, has learned how to glut you with terror, to enervate your spirit with old wives' tales and meaningless words. Come, boy, come! Knock around with us and have fun, toast with the drinkers, gamble, charm the ladies, fight, and enjoy yourself with those who gallivant, drink, gamble, charm the ladies, and enjoy themselves. Tomorrow

---

[35] This is a reference to the minor Franciscan order of the Capuchins. Capuchin friars take a vow of poverty and live austerely. This contains a hidden jab, however: veils are for nuns, not monks.

you'll be a sad retiree; old age will have stolen the pleasures of your youth, happiness will have fled twenty leagues from your domicile, and then you'll bemoan not having enjoyed these delightful moments in your present state.

"Wake up, Catrín, disabuse yourself of those falsehoods! Take it easy; enjoy yourself; gamble; charm the ladies; be what you are, that is; realize that to be a soldier, even at the rank of a private, is much more than being an employee, a judge, or a priest. An officer of the king is greater than everyone on this earth: all must respect him, and he need respect no one; civil laws were not made for soldiers, to transgress them is but a small infraction if you obey the ordinances and dress with a bit of elegance. In times of war, all goods are for the taking, even women, and in times of peace we make war anyway, putting hand to saber for any little thing. So put those words with which your uncle terrified you out of your mind and live well. Death, eternity, and honor are phantasms; they are boogeymen used to scare little children. *Death*, they say; but why should we fear death when dying is a tribute owed to nature? Man dies, the same as a dog, cat, and even a tree, and therefore there's nothing exceptional about man's death. *Eternity*; who's seen it, who's spoken to a saint or a condemned soul? It's a chimera. *Honor*; this is an elastic word that each man stretches to his liking. It's a point of honor to fight one's enemy to the death on the battlefield, it's a point of honor to slay the defenseless, to steal his goods, and abuse the innocence of his daughters. This you have seen; the fun is in being able to set the scene and dole out the parts, in having the ability to trick your superiors, and all the while passing for a wise, valiant, and prudent soldier.

"So find your honor among your comrades; be modern, generous, and soldierly, for if you take on mystical or sanctimonious airs you'll be a thorn not only in my side but in that of Precioso, Taravilla, and even Modesto, who, you know, is so good that he can scarcely break a plate."

This Modesto was a young officer who had been listening to Tremendo's speech in total silence, but he broke it at this time, saying with great seriousness:

"Listen, Tremendo, this new cadet has good reason to be confused after listening to a speech as scandalous as the one Taravilla just gave, and he will have even more reason to be confused if he decides to obey the mad ideas you have just mentioned, whose wickedness you yourself cannot grasp. Young though I may be, I do not belong to the race of the Catrines and Tremendos, and I must tell you that he does very well to heed the decent, Christian sentiments that his good uncle has inspired in him. Yes, my friend Don Catrín, understand that a military career is not a road stretching to hell. The cadet, like the officer, is a gentleman, if not by pedigree then because the king made him one on account of his merit or because the cadet pleased him. But the rogue, the libertine, the impious, the *fachenda*,[36] and the braggart are not nor will they ever have the semblance of gentlemen. No, my friend, a military career is illustrious, its ordinances and its laws are very just, and the king cannot, should not, and does not wish to authorize robbery, murder, the rape of maidens, sacrilege, incitement, trickery, *fachenda*, pride, or libertinage, which, unfortunately, is what many of my degraded companions believe. No, sir, an officer who has the distinction of serving beneath the king's flags must be gracious, self-possessed, educated, humane, religious, and he must have the conduct of a legitimate gentleman.

"The king grants you no license to offend a peaceful civilian, to trample his honor or that of his family, to swindle, or to be a shameless, rabble-rousing ruffian. And know, my friend, that when you commit these misdeeds, all your braided cords, military epaulets, medallions, and gold embroidery will only make you loathsome in the eyes of the wise and virtuous, of your commanders

---

[36] A colloquial term for haughtiness and vanity, applied to someone overly interested in his or her appearance. *Fachenda* derives from the noun *facha*, from the Latin *fascies*, "face" or "appearance." In Spanish it means "appearance" or "figure," and by extension "clothing," "suit," or "fashion."

and of the whole world, for the whole world resents the rogue's conduct, regardless of whether he may call himself a lord. In such a case, your superiors will humiliate you in public, your equals will detest you, and your inferiors will curse you.

"If a common nobody is made hateful by these vices, imagine if that nobody were also a blasphemer and a nonbeliever who rose up scandalously against our Catholic religion, the holiest, the one true and justified religion. Does it not suffice to be a violator of the law? Is it necessary to undermine dogma, to poke fun at the mysteries, and to make a barefaced mockery of that which is most sacred, on the authority of buffoons, fools, and libertines?"

"If you're referring to me," Tremendo answered very angrily, "if you're referring to me, you waster, you colossal hypocrite, you'd better watch out, because I . . . well, not even Saint Peter could make me look bad, not in this lifetime! You know me, boy: be frank, because I have a bad temper, and for the life of Pilate's cap,[37] if I get mad, with one slash of my saber I'll send you searching for your innards in the world beyond."

Everyone howled, as they were wont, at Tremendo's arrogance, but Modesto, quite serious, said to him:

---

[37] A strong statement, something like "by God's eyes I swear that . . ."

"Go on and have your fun, braggart, do you really think you frighten me with your swaggering? I am convinced that the biggest talkers are the biggest cowards."

"That's not true, by Christ," Tremendo said. "The coward and the talker is you, and here is how I'll show you . . ."

As he said this, he unsheathed his saber, and, lighter than a feather, Modesto drew his too and took a defensive position . . .

But let us leave them with their sabers in their hands and save the outcome of their fierce battle for the next chapter, for this one is becoming quite long, and the prudent reader will feel like a smoke, taking some snuff, or coughing or sneezing, and it would be unreasonable to hinder him from taking a breath.

Chapter 4

Which gives an account of the outcome of Tremendo's campaign and his challenge of Catrín, and which treats duels

The previous chapter left our two brave champions with their sabers frozen in midair, but these did not stay motionless for long. Tremendo took a furious swing that fell just short of Modesto, who escaped with a skillful side step that was both wondrous and unfortunate—unfortunate for me, because the saber glanced off my left shoulder and left its mark there.

I became vexed, as I should have, and, recalling the lessons my friends had given me about never letting anyone cross me and about evening the score after every offense, as small as it might be, and about never excusing the slightest fault committed against my respectable person, remembering, as I was saying, these and other wholesome tenets as fine and reliable as the ones bestowed on me by my friends, I lit up with rage, and, little accustomed to the use of a saber, I forgot to reach for it, and, grabbing a glass of *aguardiente* that I had before me, I threw it in Tremendo's face. But he had the good fortune of having the glass shatter on the button of his hat, and some liquor got in his eyes. Then, hopping mad from the burning, he became so incensed that he began to deliver a host of feverish slashes left and right at everything on God's green earth, and so many did the cursed madman issue that we were all alarmed for our safety.

The room was chaos; glasses, dishes, bottles, tables, and other furnishings in the café rolled on the ground as we tried to defend ourselves with chairs. The unlucky owners of the café were divided in their opinions: some wanted to get help from the men on guard, and others opposed this idea because they did not want to make it worse for themselves.

The shrieks, blows, racket, and hollering were unendurable, until finally two companions seized the opportunity to grasp Tremendo by the arms. Then they took his saber, and, putting Tremendo in the innermost room of the house, tried to calm him. This they could not accomplish, because all the rage that Tremendo had felt toward Modesto he now redirected toward me, and, shouting vows and curses, he insulted me to his pleasure, finishing by swearing on his word as a gentleman to avenge himself and clear the insult made upon his honor with sword in hand:

"Well then, if you're of noble birth," he said to me, "and if you're as brave man-to-man on the battlefield as you are in the café surrounded by your friends, I'll be waiting for you with my saber at four o'clock this afternoon in the San Lázaro cemetery. I know you won't come because you are a coward, but I'll be satisfied with your fear. My honor will preserve its brilliance, and you'll be deemed contemptible by your pals."

Saying this, he left without waiting for a response.

Everyone looked at one another with great attention and then rested their eyes on me. I understood what their astonished expressions and silence meant, and while it was as certain as death that I was terrified of Tremendo and that I would have given everything I had in my pockets for him not to have challenged me, I was ashamed for having remained silent, and, pulling myself together, I told them:

"Naturally, there's nothing to consider, my friends. I accept the duel! This afternoon we will battle each other on the field. What would they say of Don Catrín Fachenda if he showed cowardice in the first public show of honor that presented itself to him? No, by no means will I hide my face from danger. That would be rich, would it not, for a soldier who shouldn't fear an entire line of enemies to be afraid of a mincing loudmouth like Tremendo! He has two arms, just as I do, and I'm sure he has a saber as good as mine; he won't let his heart fail him, just as I won't let mine fail me. He could kill me, or I could kill him, which is the most likely scenario. I feel sorry for him, because if I hit him just right—like today's glass of *aguardiente*—they'd better start looking for a place to bury him."

There were some who could not stop laughing at my big talk, but every last one of them supported my decision to accept the duel, and I understood that everyone held me as a brave man with honor and resolve—that is, everyone with the exception of Modesto, who said to me:

"Come on, my little friend, quit your lunacy and your quixotic plan. To provoke a duel and to accept it does not prove the least bit of valor. Duels are made out of vengeance and accepted out of arrogance. Honor is found not on the point of your sword but in the orderliness of your customs. It takes more valor to pardon a grievance than to seek revenge; the whole world knows this and admires it, and history preserves thousands of examples that confirm this kind of true heroism.

"Any noble soul will stir when it hears about the generosity with which Joseph[38] in Egypt pardoned his perfidious brothers, who sold him as a slave to traders in their childhood. David[39] seems mightier when he pardons and spares the life of his enemy, Saul, than when he goes to avenge the barbaric rudeness of Abigail's husband. Alexander,[40] Caesar,[41] Marcus Aurelius,[42] and

---

[38] Joseph was one of the twelve sons of Jacob. His story is told in Genesis.

[39] David is an important figure in the Old Testament, and the bulk of his story is told in the books of Samuel. His success as a warrior troubled Saul, king of ancient Israel, who feared that David might usurp the throne. Despite Saul's attempts to kill him, David spared the king's life. After the death of Saul in battle and the execution of Saul's heir, David was proclaimed king of Israel.

[40] Alexander III of Macedon (356–323 BCE), celebrated as Alexander the Great, was the son of King Philip II. He led a series of successful and ambitious military campaigns, and his empire, while short-lived, stretched from Greece to northwest India.

[41] Gaius Julius Caesar (100–44 BCE) was a Roman governor, general, and statesman who gained fame and power during the Gallic Wars. He was proclaimed dictator for life in 49 BCE but was assassinated only a few years later by a group of nobles

[42] Marcus Aurelius (121–180) was a Roman emperor, a Stoic philosopher, and the author of the *Meditations*.

others grieved the death of their greatest enemies, the latter two regretting not having savored the glory of forgiving them. Theodosius the Younger was criticized by his people for being too humane to his enemies, to which he replied: 'In truth, far from ordering the death of my living enemies, I would like to revive the deceased ones.' What a fitting response for an emperor who merited the title!

"It would weary you, my friend, and I would risk seeming like a pedant desirous of vomiting up all his erudition at once, if I were to recount every well-known story of this sort that comes to mind: suffice it to say that to forgive an offense is more glorious than to avenge it. For this reason God said through Solomon: 'He who is slow to anger is better than the mighty, and he whose temper is controlled is better than he who captures a city.'*

"To vanquish one's enemy can be a simple coincidence, and this can be attributed to valor, skill, or good fortune; but to vanquish oneself is a sign of the honorable use of reason, of a wellspring of virtue, and of a noble soul. On no occasion do these accomplishments shine brighter than when one forgives offenses; it is then that the superiority of a great soul is unmistakable. This is

* Proverbs 16.32.

why the famous and celebrated Descartes[43] used to say: 'Whenever anyone has offended me, I try to raise my soul so high that the offense cannot reach me.' In the light of these things, consider how great was Cicero's praise of Caesar when he said that 'he forgot nothing except the wrongs done unto him.' This single expression from the lips of that Roman orator paints us a portrait of that great man.

"By contrast, the vileness and degradation of the vengeful man's heart can be seen a league away, a truth that the unenlightened gentiles discovered with the light of the Gospel. 'The desire for revenge,' said Juvenal,[44] 'is the unmistakable sign of a weak spirit and a narrow soul.'

"In most cases, the swashbucklers and the duelers are none other than the world's most wicked and ill-bred men. Ignorant of what real honor is made of, they use it as a shield behind which they take revenge and satisfy their excessive arrogance, and if this abominable conduct and disposition is detestable in citizens, it is that much more so in soldiers, who, it is assumed, should know the meaning of true honor and understand those lessons

---

[43] René Descartes (1596–1650) was a French mathematician, philosopher, and scientist. He is credited as having initiated the philosophical movement of rationalism.

[44] Decimus Junius Juvenalis, known simply as Juvenal, was a famous Roman poet who wrote at the end of the first and the beginning of the second century CE. The verses quoted here come from *Satire 13*.

that teach us to be attentive, kind, and prudent with everyone.

"With reason Theodoric[45] wrote to his quarrelsome soldiers: 'Take up your arms against your enemies, and do not use them against one another. May trivial arguments never lead you to reprehensible excesses. Submit yourselves to the justice that brings universal happiness. Forsake the iron when the state has no enemies, for it is a great crime to take arms against citizens, in whose defense it is glorious to risk one's life.'

"I know, my companions, that I must have displeased you with my long speech, but be understanding, for all my efforts are made in hopes that Don Catrín will abstain from the duel and realize that doing so will not harm the good standing he has earned among us in the least."

"That can't be," I said, "for Tremendo would consider it cowardly and contemptible."

"The alternative would be to accept the duel," Modesto answered me, "in which case you will be contemptible in the eyes of the law and excommunicated by the church, which will even deny your corpse a holy resting place if you die in combat.

---

[45] Theodoric the Great (454–526) was king of the Ostrogoths during the waning years of the Roman Empire.

"As a new soldier, you have yet to see the pragmatism behind this, but by good fortune I have in my pocket the third volume of the *Military Ordinances*,[46] which I will read to you in its entirety, even if you do not want me to, so that you cannot allege your ignorance or blame me if I inform on you, which is what will happen if you go through with the duel to which you have been challenged. Listen carefully.

"'Don Philip . . . etc.'"

Here he read the entire document to us, down to the last letter, and then he proceeded.

"The wholesome intentions of this law and its benefits to humanity cannot be clearer. Spain is not alone in deeming abominable the accursed practice of duels, born in a past age among barbarous and fierce nations of the north. In the sixteenth century, Gustavus Adolphus,[47] who was the first conqueror who tried to bring the northern peoples to the superior civilization, realizing that duels had begun to damage his army, banned them under penalty of death. It so happens, says Abbot

---

[46] Legislation related to the Spanish military that was passed in 1632 under Philip IV and that subsequent rulers modified. The version that would have been in force during the era represented in the novel was passed in 1768, during the reign of Charles III.

[47] King of Sweden from 1611 to 1632 credited for transforming Sweden into a major European power.

Blanchard,[48] that a dispute arose between two of the king's most important officers, and they requested the king's permission to battle each other man-to-man. The king became vexed straightaway at the proposition; however, he acquiesced, adding that he wished to be a witness at the duel. The king set out with a small infantry that, when it arrived, encircled the two brave men. The king then said to the two rivals: 'Come on, men, be strong and fight until one of you falls dead.' Then he turned, called to the army's executioner, and said: 'The moment that one of the two falls dead, cut off the other one's head in my presence.' This was enough to make both men, who recognized their foolish pride, implore the king for forgiveness, which forever reconciled the two men and imparted a lasting lesson to Sweden, where there was no more mention of duels in the army from that time forward."

"Phew, what a sentence!" said Taravilla. "Now that's a game no one could win! But it can't be denied that the

---

[48] Jean-Baptiste Blanchard was a French Jesuit and academic and the author of *L'Ecole des moers* (1782; *The School of Manners*). Lizardi borrowed several narratives from this book for *Don Catrín*, including the story of the seventeenth-century Swedish king who lectured his soldiers on the evils of dueling (ch. 4). Blanchard's text also provided the comic tale in chapter 8 that recounts how a French writer, driven insane by excessive alcohol, attempted to orchestrate a mass suicide, and how the French playwright Molière cleverly tricked him out of it.

king's intention was good, for he didn't want either man to die."

With that, our session came to an end, for the clock struck two in the afternoon and every one of us needed to go home to eat.

I went home, but I ate with uneasiness, for I took everything that Modesto had said as cowardice, and, resolved to honor the duel, I jumped into bed to pass the *siesta*,[49] but I did not sleep, for I had my eye on the clock.

When it struck three-thirty I rose instantly, and taking my saber, left in the direction of San Lázaro. There I met Tremendo, and we fought and were friends once more, as you will see in the chapter that follows.

Chapter 5

Long, but very interesting

I found Tremendo strolling about the San Lázaro cemetery. The sight of him, his massive frame, his large moustaches, and the solitude of the place scared me so much that my knees shook, and I nearly turned back more

---

[49] A short nap taken after the midday meal. It is still observed by some inhabitants of Spain and areas once belonging to the Spanish Empire.

than once; but he had seen me, and I could not allow my honor to diminish in his opinion.

Deliberating on the situation, and repeating to myself that fortune favors the bold, that he who strikes first wins, and that in these situations one should either resolve to die or kill his enemy with the first blow, I approached Tremendo with my saber unsheathed, declaring when I was twelve paces away:

"Defend yourself, coward, because hell is about to come tumbling down on you!"

The yell with which I pronounced these words, the boldness with which I charged forward, the immeasurable slashes, reverses, and thrusts that I threw without system, the absolute incompetency with which he handled his sword, and my tenacious resolution to die so overwhelmed Tremendo that he never attacked me but simply tried to defend himself.

"Calm down, boy," he said, "calm down: this was all just a prank to test you and measure your courage, but I'm your friend and I don't want a real fight."

By his words I took it that he was confessing my superior skill as a swordsman; but, remembering that the winner's luck can change in a moment, and that terror occasionally produces prodigious feats of bravery, as it had just done with me, I resolved to give in, for my honor was in good shape and the formidable Tremendo was surrendering.

I took three steps back, and in a deeply solemn tone, I said:

"I'll stop fighting because you pronounce your friendship, but for the future, don't risk your life so recklessly."

Tremendo ratified his affection for me once again, both of us swore on our lives not to tell a soul about what had come to pass between us, we sheathed our sabers, threw our arms around each other, kissed each other on the cheek, and went to the café very happy. And that is how our terrible duel ended.

On the way, I told him everything that Modesto had said about duels, about his claim that the *riotous* and *uncontrollable* soldiers and knights who challenged, accepted, or in any way participated in duels faced treason and seizure of their belongings, and that, if two men resolved to duel, no matter if it did not end in fighting, death, or injury, but if it were verified that they simply met on the battlefield, they would be punished, *without any attenuations*, by death.

"I knew all this before," Tremendo told me, "and that's why I wanted to stop the fight without injuring you, for if not—Lord save you!—when you made that thrust to the left, I would have sent your head flying to the horns of Capricorn. But I'm your friend, my honor is unimpeachable, and I only challenged you as a prank to see if you were a boy of valor. Now that I know you are, I'll be your lifelong friend, and we'll cower from nothing, not even from the furies of hell. But I must warn you: bestow your friendship on no other but me, Precioso, Taravilla, Tronera, and others like us; and under no circumstances on Modesto, Prudencio, Constante, Moderato, or any other hypocritical and foolish officers that unfortunately abound in our regiment.

"These foolish whelps, deluded by friars, will preach to you like apostolic missionaries and fill your head with somber ideas and despairing thoughts. But don't be a dimwit; arm yourself with cheerful companions like me if you want to live a life of joy free of afflictions."

Occupied with these holy discussions, we arrived at the café. Our chums were overjoyed to see us, for, as they had witnessed the challenge between us and had not seen us in the afternoon, they imagined we had cut each other to pieces out on the field.

They asked us about the outcome of our duel, and Tremendo responded that it was nothing more than a prank, for he had never had the intention of fighting me in cold blood. Everyone was pleased with the success of our duel, and, after having coffee, we each went our separate way.

For two years I lived contentedly, learning a thousand delicate skills and strategies from Tremendo and our companions. His maxims were gospel to me, and his example was the pattern on which I modeled my customs.

In a matter of days I dedicated myself to being soldierly, to entertaining myself with skirts and playing
cards, to yielding to no one, regardless of who they were,
to speaking freely about matters of state and religion, to
becoming rich by any means possible, and to other activities of this nature, which are of the highest importance
to soldiers such as I.

The deluded officers Modesto, Justo, Moderato, and
other such fanatics tormented me at every instant with
their pestering sermons, insisting that the maxims I was
adopting and the customs I sought to imitate were flawed
and scandalous; that in time I would be nothing more
than a shameless, insolent, blasphemous lout, a libertine,
gambler, instigator, and cheat; that with each grade that
one earned in the service of the king, one had that much
more obligation to be a gentleman and a good Christian,
for the crimes that bring imprisonment or caning upon
the common private beget more serious sentences for the
cadet or the officer, for it is supposed that these are en-
dowed with higher principles and greater enlightenment,
and, by consequence, greater honor and obligations.

They told me this and a thousand similar things, and I
was told the contrary by my friends, who said that the fanatics' words were hogwash, hypocrisy, and deceitful talk.

"Howl with the wolves," Taravilla told me. "You don't
believe that the magistrate's laws, the friar's rules, or

the guild's statutes are the same thing as military ordinances, do you? Don't believe it even if they swear it's
true. Just as in his dress, the soldier should differ in his
practices from the lawyer, the friar, the office worker, the
laborer, the artisan, the merchant, the clergyman, and
every sort of civilian. Is there any pleasure equal to that
of seducing a married woman, deceiving a virgin, stab-
bing a fanatic who considers himself upright and proper
and laughing at his notion of justice, swindling a miser,
mocking a hypocrite, and lecturing on things about
which we have no understanding? Come on, Catrín,
you've seen very little, and you have no notion of the enlightened era in which you live. Laugh, laugh a thousand
and one times at the stupidities of some of our officers,
who with their foolishness try to make you a Capuchin
monk with braided cords on your shoulders. It is true
that everyone in the regiment likes them, that their superiors appreciate them, that dopey civilians open their
doors to them, and that their pride is swollen by these rewards. But in reality, what are these men but underlings
who appease the appetites of tedious saints and moral-
ists? No, my friend, don't confine yourself to such narrow
limits. Spread your wings, broaden your horizons, make
merry in the way of those who call themselves *libertines*:
may there be no woman who doesn't fall victim to your
conquest, no purse safe from your snare, no virtue free

from your guile, no religion or law that isn't obliterated by your tongue, aided as it is by your inestimable talent, and you'll be the honor of the Catrines and the glory of your homeland."

As my heart has always been very docile, I took great advantage of these lessons. I pooh-poohed the troublesome preachers and gave myself over entirely to pleasure. Two years went by in this way—and ah, what two years they were, the happiest one could imagine!

Within a few days, thanks to the wholesome advice and edifying examples of my friends, I spoke twenty sinful things for every honorable word I said, I poked fun at religion and its ministers, and trickery and double-dealing seemed nothing less than points of honor to me, as opposed to acts of necessity.

If the first year was good, then what followed was undeniably perfect, for at the beginning of the second year my father took a shine to the idea of dying, and he got his way; my mother did not have it in her to be alone, and within a month's time she went to accompany him in the graveyard.

Incredible was my delight upon finding myself free from that old pair of moaners, for, though it is true they loved me very much and never opposed my ideas, they weighed me down in some way that I cannot explain with their meekness and their wrinkled faces. It is true that some evil tongues said I killed them with the troubles I caused, but that is just the calumny of mean-spirited people, for I have always behaved respectably, as you have all seen and will continue to see in the course of my life.

My parents left me some small treasures: clothing, furniture, and about five hundred pesos in cash, for which I was never thankful, since, having no way to take it with them, it was inevitable that they leave it to their good son.

Once the nine days had passed,[50] my house was transformed into a veritable Arcadia.[51] My friends and relatives the Catrines paid me endless visits, lunches and gambling were customary, and *tertulias* were the preferred nightly entertainment. These were attended by my pals, both military men and civilians, and a swarm of young women, ordinary and genteel, the majority of whom had titles, though none from Castile. In short, the women sang, danced, and satisfied our every whim.

It goes without saying that I shelled out for most of the expenses, and while I noticed that my cash was rid-

---

[50] A reference to the nine days of mourning in Christianity called the *novena*.

[51] *Arcadia* conjures images of idyllic, natural spaces distant from the frenetic activities of the city, images that contrast greatly with the situation Don Catrín goes on to describe.

ing away from me like a horse at the races, I was not concerned, for my friends told me that I was very liberal and generous, that I was lacking money but that I had an excellent hand.

In the midst of this praise, I was bled dry, and for a trifle of four or five months' rent that I owed, my landlord presented himself to my colonel and succeeded in clearing out the house, and with that, the fun ended at once.

An earthenware pitcher and an old chest were the only furniture that I took, for the other pieces, which were few and bad, were left because of the debt. I took refuge at Taravilla's, which was a tiny house in a poor neighborhood.

It was at this stage that my hardships began, for neither he nor I had a *real* between us. Procuring our daily bread was the least of our troubles, for we made many visits, and we nibbled at some, lunched or dined at others, and sometimes took coffee with friends. On the other hand, living without the luxuries indispensable to our class was unbearable, especially for me, who counted on a salary of no more than eleven pesos, and with that I could not even afford a pair of boots.

In the midst of this consternation, I spied on a neighboring balcony a girl of about nineteen years, bony, pasty, with two missing teeth, a Roman nose, and a mole the size of a swollen chickpea.

As she was dressed very decently and in a large house, I greeted her to see what might come of it, and she responded with delight.

Her affection did not flatter me tremendously on account of her bad looks; but later, upon relating the incident to my companion, he said to me:

"You should pray to God that she's fond of you! In that case your happiness would be sealed, for that ugly girl is the daughter of Don Abundo, a flush old man, and since she was born he's been giving her a thousand pesos a year, which means that she's as many thousands rich as she is old. It would do for you to marry her even if she were fifty years old, for she would bring you fifty thousand pesos. Withal, nineteen or twenty thousand pesos aren't bundles of hay, so make it happen, don't be foolish."

Encouraged by such favorable news, I dedicated myself to courting her unscrupulously. My strolls down her street were frequent, and she always returned my greetings with satisfaction.

I came to write her, and she wrote to me, and each time I would send a maidservant with oranges, a kerchief with grapes, or other similar gifts, for I could give nothing better. She accepted them with affection and corresponded liberally. On one occasion, she sent me a parcel of cambric linen, and on another, a box of gold dust.

Such practices left me more in love each day, and I considered her in my pocket. It is certain that her dreadful body and even worse face were repugnant to me, but what would one not overlook (said I to my tailcoat) for twenty thousand pesos? With one or two thousand, I could buy her as much pleasure as she desired, bury her in a year, and have eighteen for my own use.

With these thoughts in mind, I brought up the subject of marriage to her, which she accepted, adding, however, that I should discuss it with her father through a respectable intermediary.

But I was too aware of my merit to resort to ambassadors who could bring my arrangement to ruin, and so I went by myself and told her father my saintly intentions face-to-face.

The old dog heard me with great calm, then he replied:

"My young friend, I am truly obliged to you for loving my daughter to the degree that you describe, but have you seen her? She is quite ugly, and if I her father can see this, how can it be that you do not?

"Nature has denied her graces, but fortune has furnished her with assets. She has coinage enough to get by without marrying, enough even to make herself tolerable to a good husband, if it be her volition to marry. If God sees fit that you be the one, by all means you will be; but it is imperative that you do not rush, so that you both have more time to examine your inclination."

With these few words the old man bid me farewell, telling me to return in one month's time to tell him how I felt about his daughter. I was despondent, but I was forced to go along with it.

Meanwhile, I discovered that he began to inform himself little by little of who I was and the nature of my conduct, which did not please him, for when I returned to see him he received me with disgust, stating resolutely that he would not give his daughter to a man of my circumstances, for he did not think to make her unhappy.

I boiled inside at such a biting response, unfit for an eminent gentleman such as I, and I vowed to avenge myself of Don Abundo by stealing his daughter. I proposed that she and I elope together, she agreed, and we arranged a plan. On the night destined for the escape, I entered the house, climbed into a coach that was in the courtyard, and sent word to Sinforosa, for that was the beak-nosed girl's name.

In a few minutes, she came down with a little trunk of treasures and money, but alas, I only had the pleasure of feeling its weight. There we were inside the coach, waiting for the right moment to make our getaway, when all of a sudden who should appear but the damned old man with a pistol in his hand, accompanied by a servant carrying a lantern shining abundant light.

Each of them took hold of the coach reins, and the old man glared at his daughter with the look of a snake that had been stepped on. Turning in the direction of his servant, he said:

"Take this crazy girl into the house and do what I have ordered."

At this, the beak-nosed girl, now crying, stepped down from the coach and went away with the servant.

Once the old man and I were left alone, he ordered:

"Leave here, vile seducer, get out."

I did not have the slightest desire to exit the coach; I do not know where my gusto was hiding. That devil of an old man saw my reluctance to fight, and taking advantage of what he believed was fear, he grabbed me by my shirt, gave me two or three tugs, and with a fierce pull tore me from the seat and sent me flying to the ground, where I lay disheveled, crawling on all fours.

Seeing myself abused by an old codger like him, I tried to reach for my sword, but what strength that shriveled-up old man had! In no time, he dragged me to my feet against my will with another tremendous yank. This time I told him:

"Be warned, my friend, and do not treat me this way, for I am a cadet and one step away from becoming a soldier, and what is more, I am the gentleman Don Catrín, noble and illustrious on each of my four sides. While I may respect your gray hair for now, tomorrow I am going to collect my letters patent of nobility and family trees, and then you will understand who I am and that destroying you is as easy as drawing a good card."

The old dog grew intimidated at this; that or he grew tired of kicking me. What I know for certain is that he let me go, saying:

"Go, and may the devil take you, you rogue, you shameless scoundrel. A gentleman, my foot! If you were noble, you would not act with infamy. Ah, but you have just told me who you are! Don Catrín . . . yes, I already know about the Catrines. Leave, get out of my sight before I empty this pistol into you."

To avoid complications, I left. I did not want to relay the shameful incident to my companion, for he would think that my actions had been the result not of great prudence but of great cowardice, and he would be dismayed to see that he who had defied Tremendo's sword was afraid of a worthless old mumblecrust.

On the inside, however, I swore to avenge myself and, if necessary, to bring a company of grenadiers to this effect.

Such were my intentions. As these are often thwarted, however, so mine were in an instant on the following day.

At eight o'clock in the morning, at which hour I did not dream of rising from bed, an army orderly came knocking at the door. When he was let in by my companion, the orderly told me that the colonel expected to see me within half an hour.

Believing the colonel had summoned me in order to promote me to second lieutenant, I dressed myself cheerfully and set off to see him.

The colonel received me with a sour expression on his face and said:

"Did you suppose that being a soldier is the same as being a rogue, with neither law nor king? I cannot tolerate any more complaints about your bad conduct, and I have tried everything that my position requires in order to help you.

"It has all been in vain; far from reforming yourself, fulfilling your academy duties and attending assemblies, distancing yourself from bad friends and behaving like an honorable officer, you have done nothing but abuse my prudence, shock the virtuous, outstrip the scoundrels in unruliness, and tomorrow you would pervert my most upstanding men.

"You recall last night's episode; I will not go into it because it will make me ashamed. I cannot allow nor do I want such a barefaced and insolent pest like you in my regiment. And so, request your resignation in the next three days; if you do not do this, you subject yourself to public humiliation and dishonorable discharge from the regiment. So, do what you wish, and go with God."

Saying this, he took his hat and cane and left, leaving me without a chance to reply.

Full of confusion, I left his house and went to mine. I consulted with my companions about my troubles, and they all advised me to request my resignation, for, if I did not, the colonel would shame me in public and would keep his eye on me until he managed to throw me out—by way of ordinance—for immoral behavior and for being beyond hope of reform.

It was unpleasant for me to humble myself and follow through with this course of action, but realizing that if I liked I could leave the regiment, and if I did not I would get kicked out, I made the decision to leave before anything else might come to pass.

With this determination, I petitioned for my resignation, which was granted speedily, and lo and behold, I was a civilian once again, a transformation that pleased me not a bit. But there was nothing to be done except conform to the new situation and follow my career wherever it might lead.

And this I did, and this you will see in the telling of this great, sublime, and true story.

CHAPTER 6

IN WHICH IT WILL BE SEEN HOW LADY
FORTUNE BEGAN TO PERSECUTE HIM, AND THE
TACTICS HE ADOPTED TO OUTWIT HER

Hardly did I feel the fresh air meet my face—not as a student, soldier, businessman, laborer, artisan, or anything of the sort, but as a civilian, plain and simple—when my officer friends turned their backs on me.

No one paid me the slightest compliment, and they did not even bother to acknowledge me; this owed perhaps to the fact that I did not have a single peso to my name, having spent the profits I made selling my uniform in a single visit to the Parián,[52] where I bought a blue tailcoat, a round hat, a pair of resoled boots, a watch

---

[52] A market in the busy center of Mexico City built in the early eighteenth century. It was destroyed during a riot in 1828 and was finally demolished during the government of General Santa Anna in 1843 (González Obregón 407).

for thirty coins, a chain of the latest fashion, a little cane, and a handkerchief.

I still had two shirts, two pairs of pants, two waist-coats, and two white handkerchiefs, thanks to which I could present myself with some decency.

My comrade Taravilla dismissed me politely from his house, saying he could no longer have me by his side in the light of what everyone was saying about me—though between you and me, he talked more than anyone else did on the subject. In any case, he told me:

"You see, brother, the colonel has a poor opinion of you, and if he knew that you lived with me, he'd think I was just like you; he wouldn't let me out of his sight, and that would be the end of my promotions. So come on, pal, clear out before the end of today."

I understood—for I have quite a talent for discern-ment—that he was afraid to lose what little favor he had left with the colonel; I decided that he was only too right, and so I took a little room on Mesones Street for twelve *reales*. I said goodbye to Taravilla and moved my things in a single trip.

Alone in my house, with adequate clothing and a sense of decency, I was quite happy, when all of a sud-den I remembered that I did not even have enough for breakfast the next day. Thus pursued by old hardships, I fell back on old methods. Entering a café, I took a seat at a table. A young man came over to ask what I would be having, and I answered that I would have nothing until a friend I was expecting arrived.

In effect, the first person to arrive was a friend of mine, for I began to adulate him so eagerly and with such charm, that he, gratified, offered me some coffee, and I did not make him beg.

I told him a thousand lies straightaway, affirming that of all my troubles, what pained me the most was having a young and comely sister who had to remain under my care while she waited to receive an inheritance that belonged to her. I deftly added that, in addition to being her brother, I was authorized to represent her and act in her name, that according to our lawyer the situation augured well, and that in a matter of two months more than six thousand pesos would be coming our way. When that happens, I told my new friend, I will pay off some small debts that I owe and find her a respectable husband. Whether he is rich or poor does not matter, as long as his blood is as good as mine, which should not be difficult, for, as you know, the brood of the Catrines is as plentiful as it is illustrious.

"That is no secret to me," answered my friend, "for I belong to the same race, a fact that pleases me so much that I would not change places with the noblest man in the whole world."

Then, rising from my seat and clasping him in a formidable embrace, I said to him:

"I rejoice at this felicitous meeting, which has introduced me to a new family member."

"It is I who have the pleasure of meeting you, my good sir," he replied, paying me a thousand compliments and offering himself and his services to me. He pledged eternal friendship and insisted heartily that I ask him for anything I needed, for, as a legitimate Catrín, relative, friend, and comrade of mine, he had all that he could want.

Not content with the affection that he lavished upon me, he had them bring us *aguardiente*, and in abundance. We drank merrily, and once the harsh liquor dispatched its sprightly spirits to his head, he began to tell me his life story, and with such naivety and simplicity that before long I learned that he was a man of irreprehensible character, a rich and illustrious gentleman and useful member of society . . . In short, he was just like me, and as *pares cum paribus facile congregantur*,[53] or, put another way, as birds of a feather flock together, once I was satisfied that I knew him to his core, I pledged my friendship

---

[53] "Equals with equals easily come together."

and assured him that I would place all my affairs in his hands.

He expressed his gratitude with more *aguardiente*, and from that toast forward, we addressed each other familiarly,[54] and in this way we sealed our friendship.

At this time, there appeared at the entrance of the café four or five polished young fellows turned out in tailcoats, cravats, and leather purses. Some looked very respectable, and others looked respectable without the *very*.

They all entered and greeted Simplicio, which was my new friend's name, and they treated him with great familiarity and me with great civility. They sat down at our table and drank from our glasses, and I understood right away that they were my people.

I glowed with joy to see how numerous my brood was, for everywhere I went, I came across Catrines as good as I.

We all became friends at that moment. One of them, dispensing with tiresome overtures, said to Simplicio:

"Come on, brother! Tell them to bring us some lunch, for you're flush and we're broke. Today you do something for me, tomorrow I do something for you."

---

[54] In the source text, Don Catrín refers to the practice of using the informal mode of address, called *tutear* in Spanish.

Simplicio was generous, he had money, and as such it was not necessary to insist. He ordered lunch, and we allowed our stomachs to be fully satisfied, especially I, who lunched greedily in case I could not find anywhere to eat that afternoon.

Once lunch had ended and our friends had bid us farewell, Simplicio asked if I would bring him to my house so that he could meet my sister, if I deemed him a gentleman worthy of my friendship, that is.

And therein lay my predicament, for I had neither a sister nor anything resembling one. I had no choice but to say that I was pleased by his request, and that I would naturally grant it had I not drank so much *aguardiente*, for my sister and I lived with a very scrupulous aunt, who, if she smelled it on me, would scold me with such severity that it would embarrass me greatly. What was worse, she would presume that my new friend was to blame, taking him for a scoundrel who passed his time drunk in the streets and making a drunkard of her nephew, and for these reasons it would be better for him to meet my sister the next day. Simplicio agreed eagerly, for it seemed to him that my beautiful sister and the lawsuit that she was soon to win were already in his grasp, and that he would marry her and have three or four thousand pesos to throw around.

I saw how well my ruse had worked, and I tried to take it one step further.

Naturally, I told him that, on account of his pleasant company, I had lost the morning and had nothing to take to my house and asked if he could lend me a couple of pesos if I left him my watch.

"Get out of here!" he cried. "Am I to accept an article from a friend, relative, and comrade whom I so esteem? Take the two pesos and whatever else you might need."

Gleefully pocketing my two coins, I arranged to meet him the next morning in the same café, and we parted ways.

I did not eat anything because I did not want to break my two pesos, and to pass the time I went to a pool hall, where to my good fortune there was a clumsy, blundering player, from whom I won five pesos.

At four o'clock in the afternoon, I left to search among my old acquaintances for a girl who would like to be my sister and some crone who could play the part of my aunt.

In vain did I make the rounds through my shadowy haunts: none of my female friends would do me the favor, no matter how many pleasing brushstrokes I used to describe the situation. All of them were afraid that I was trying to play a trick on them.

Tired from walking and desperate to bring my plan to fruition, I determined to go drink some *chocolate,*[55] which I did.

There I was drinking it, when in walked an old woman accompanied by a girl, not lowbred and not at all bad-looking. They sat down at the little table where I was sitting and greeted me with great courtesy; I ordered everything they wanted for them, and the result was that I got what I wanted: the young girl agreed to be my sister and the good old woman to be my aunt.

It goes without saying that the two women were very delicate and pious and would never suspect a gentleman such as I of abusing such close family ties, and therefore they had no misgivings about offering me their house, and I accepted the honor of enjoying their good company.

They wanted to go to the Coliseum;[56] I took them, and at the end of the comedy, we went to dine and then to their house.

---

[55] For Mexicans who could afford the popular beverage, *chocolate,* or hot chocolate, was consumed in the morning with breakfast. Wealthier Mexicans often enjoyed an additional cup in the afternoon, following the *siesta* (Wasserman 143–44).

[56] A theater house that was located inside the Hospital Real de Naturales, or Royal Hospital of Natural Peoples. (In the Spanish colonies, the word *natural* was often used to describe someone born to unmar-

Countless people greeted them in the streets, at the theater, and in the tavern, addressing them with great familiarity, and I felt a surge of pride at having met such a beautiful and highly regarded sister.

At last we arrived at their house, and I was not at all surprised to find that this was a squalid little appendage of another house, and that the only furniture they had was a sofa, a *petate*,[57] a *memela*,[58] a dirty mattress, and a small adobe stove on which were the remains of some burnt beans in a cheap pot.

I was well aware that for all the splendor and luxury with which ladies of this class may present themselves, their houses and furnishings are rarely the more respectable for it.

I went into the house very contented, and my good aunt would not hear of me sleeping on the sofa because it

---

ried parents; here, however, it refers to indigenous people.) This hospital for destitute indigenous people was operated by the Hippolyte religious order. The proceeds of the theater went to financing the hospital. The building burned down and was rebuilt several times (Olvarría y Ferrari 19–32).

[57] Derived from the Nahuatl word *pétatl*, a *petate* is a mat woven from palm leaves, the most common sleeping arrangement of the lower classes. The dead were often buried in their *petate*.

[58] *Memela*, another Nahuatl word, is a food staple, a thick corn tortilla common since pre-Columbian times. In the text, it refers figuratively to one of the women's effects, possibly a round cushion or blanket that looks like a *memela*.

had too many bedbugs. And so, despite my reservations, I accompanied my sister, for I did not want them to think me rude or uncivilized.

That night I taught my sister the part that we were all to play with Simplicio, and I moved them into my house the next day, after having paid the fourteen *reales* that they owed in rent at their previous house.

After I left them in my room, I went out to meet my dearest friend, whom I found beside himself on account of my tardiness.

We had coffee and went to the house, where Simplicio was affectionately received by my lonely sister, who painted him such convincing pictures of imminent wealth and present miseries that, his compassion and avarice excited, he gave her five pesos on that first visit; then he left.

She fell completely in love with Simplicio's liberality, as he did with Laura's beauty, for Laura was her name.

Simplicio returned that afternoon and, one thing leading to another, they began to discuss getting married as soon as the lawsuit was won. With this understanding, they began to refer to each other as husband and wife, which seemed wrong neither to me nor to my aunt, for we did not see anything wrong with them rolling around with each other and going out and amusing themselves; in the end, they were two young people. Simplicio footed the bills, and we all profited from the poor fellow's liberality.

For two months, scarcely more, I lived a life that the laziest and most extravagant of men would envy; I had an aunt who waited on me and a pretty sister who pampered me, I ate well, slept until the afternoon, and did no work of any kind, which was the best part.

What is more, I never entered the cafés with fewer than four *reales* in my purse, and I was the benefactor of Simplicio's almost new scraps and leftovers, for, in addition to being wild about Laura and generous, he was the son of a well-heeled mother as doting as mine, and she indulged him in everything.

Naturally, Laura did not let her attention wander from her enterprise, and neither did my prudent aunt. We were all content and not badly supplied in clothing—but, oh!, evil, malicious tongues! Simplicio related everything about his future bride to Pedro Sagaz, a friend and relative of mine who, now eager to meet my sister, begged Simplicio to take him to her house when I was not there.

And that is what that half-wit Simplicio did; but no sooner did that good-for-nothing Sagaz recognize Laura than he turned to Simplicio and cried:

"You brutish, foolish idiot! And you consider yourself a martial, roguish, modern, seasoned Catrín? This is a well-known harlot, the daughter of the deceased Master Simon, who had his barbershop in the Plaza del

Volador.[59] Not even in her wildest dreams does she have blood ties to Catrín and much less lawsuits over money, which she never knew until her present trade.

"Catrín's a sponger and he's employed these hussies to scam you, and if you don't take care, between the three of them you'll be left without a shirt."

Upon hearing this denunciation, which Laura and the crone's silence confirmed as true, Simplicio became so enraged that he seized them, dealt them a good many blows, and, not satisfied with this, threatened them with jail on his way out.

The poor women feared what was coming and moved out that very instant. They took their furniture with them but had the generosity to leave mine, although these were in such a state that they were not even worth stealing.

They left me an explanation of what had happened, the key to the room, and moved out in one trip.

Scarcely had they left when I arrived and learned of the recent episode, for the landlady told me everything; fearing that the innocent would pay for the sins of the guilty, I paid what I owed in rent, called a carrier, and moved into the first room that I found.

---

[59] A plaza that became an important commercial center during the viceregal era. It served as a venue for diverse events over the years, including inquisitorial autos-da-fé, meetings between fruit and bean merchants, and even bullfights (González Obregón 285–92).

In this manner did our happy days end; I found myself without a sister, aunt, or friend, and my troubles began once more.

As hunger began to gnaw at me, and as I could not manage to get a cup of *chocolate*, a bite to eat, etc. by pretending I was an orphan, I was forced to sell the hand-me-downs that Simplicio had given me. But, good God!, how those shopkeepers exasperated me with their stinginess and their meanness! On an item that was worth ten pesos they would finally agree, after protracted griping and moaning, to offer twelve *reales*, and this was only when they were in the mood, for when they did not feel like dancing, I was left empty-handed—that is, except for my item.

As the situation demanded that I live by my own means, and as I could find no one who would provide for me, before I knew it I was left without a scrap to cover myself. I realize that I would have come out a little better if I had pawned and sold my baubles myself, but this could not be. A Don Catrín de la Fachenda, pawning and selling his effects with his own hands? Such conduct would have withered my honor and given fodder to my enemies and to the slanderers of my lineage.

It was absolutely necessary to employ lowbred folks for these undertakings. And how did this go? If they sold an item for six pesos, they told me they only received four; some simply took the item and left for good; others pawned my clothing and I never saw it again. And so, in a few days, as I have said, I was worse off than before I found Simplicio; from day to night I had no need for a laundry woman, for I had no shirt, and this was a concern for a gentleman such as I.

Utterly distraught to see myself in a torn tailcoat with patches on the elbows; faded *coleta*[60] pants; a broken waistcoat, but of very soft cotton; a tattered, grimy hat; and resoled boots that were so old that when I walked the bottoms flopped open like the jaws of a lizard . . . as I was saying, utterly distraught for the reasons I have just given, and because I had nothing to eat and no house to visit—for those dressed in rags have no place in the world—I decided to take the advice of my friends and make use of my talents. I resolved to become a gambler, for the issue was to find a means to eat, drink, gallivant, and have money without working at anything, for all that business about working is for ordinary folk. Gambling could provide everything at once, and so there was nothing to do but adopt this course of action.

This I did, and I will relate the results, but in a separate chapter.

------

[60] A rough linen that was used to make everyday garments.

Chapter 7

He sets out to become a gambler, and notable
incidents that befall him during his career

You all know, dear companions, that in this sad life, good and evil are like links in a chain, with one leading to the next, and there is no one who is consistently happy or consistently wretched.

It was in this period of my life that I learned firsthand the accuracy of this maxim, or whatever it is. I resolved to become a gambler, but how to proceed? With what principle, if I had no money and didn't know a soul who would lend me a bag of scorpions on credit? However, I did not lose spirit; I went to the first gaming house that presented itself and planted myself behind the *monte*[61] dealer, who wasn't very bright, and every now and then I would bend down as if I were going to adjust my boots, and on one of these occasions I saw that he had a great hand.

I then advised or "gave a nudge" to someone who was close by; I had the good fortune of his believing me, and he bet all the money he had and all he had borrowed,

---

[61] *Monte* is a card game in which several players bet on the cards the dealer will pull from the deck. The game originated in Spain and was later introduced in the Americas.

won about two hundred pesos from the sorry dealer, and cleverly slipped me six on the sly. I ingratiated myself with the players and had the pleasure of collecting sixty pesos that afternoon. It is true that "some small maneuvers" were involved, and that I also benefited from the good harmony that developed between everyone.

I went to the Parián immediately and bought two percale shirts, a very reasonable tailcoat, and all the items necessary for the adornment of my person, without forgetting the watch, little cane, powders, combs, creams, monocle, and gloves, for all this is indispensable to gentlemen of my class. I paid a driver a nice bonus to take these items to my house, and that afternoon I fixed myself up properly, getting dressed, arranging my hair, and perfuming myself, and I took to the street with fifteen pesos that I had left over. I walked into a café to have some coffee, and the first person I saw was Simplicio, who, amazed at my sudden respectability, not only spared me a severe tongue-lashing about what had happened but asked me very amicably about the provenance of my happy prosperity.

"My sister's lawsuit has been won," I answered somewhat seriously.

"Your sister?"

"Yes, sir, my sister, that unhappy woman who had the misfortune of having loved you."

"But Sagaz . . ."

"Yes, Sagaz is an utter rogue; seeing that my sister did not favor him, he took his revenge by filling your head with gossip . . . Let us speak no more of this, or I will boil over."

Simplicio then gave me a thousand reasons for his actions and asked me where she lived, and I replied that she was living on her estate while her wedding was being prepared.

"What do you mean her wedding?" Simplicio asked, turning pale. I continued my trick with great subtlety, until he believed it completely.

"Damn Sagaz!" he said, full of rage. "He has forever robbed me of my happiness."

I almost let out a shriek of laughter upon seeing how easily I had once again duped him. I offered him some coffee, and, upon paying, I made as much noise as I could with my fifteen pesos. At last we said goodbye, and he went to the Coliseum and I to the gaming house.

I passed several good days, thanks to Birján's books,[62] for as everyone saw me looking decent, they thought I must have a lot to lose, and for this most honest of

---

[62] *Birján* is another spelling of *Vilhan*, whom many believed to have invented playing cards and card tricks. Rinconete, a protagonist in one of Miguel de Cervantes's *Novelas ejemplares* (*Exemplary Novels*), refers to this figure (Aylward 73).

reasons they gave me the best place at every table. But I was never more than what one would call a dabbler and was satisfied with the little I needed to get by; as soon as I won two or three pesos, I would bury them in my pocket, take out my cigar, and go out to smoke it.

It is well known that fortune wearies of favoring one person for very long, and thus, it will surprise no one that it took flight in two weeks' time, and my old hardships returned with greater force.

As everyone knew that I was poor, the sharpers lessened their courtesies. Poverty obliged me to pull a few stunts, and in a few of these incidents I had to deliver and suffer some blows in order to uphold the honor of my word; I was in a wretched state for some time until, to top it all off, the law surprised me one night, and I had the honor of going to jail for the first time.

Since I did not have the money to pay the fine, I was forced to endure prison, where in order to eat I was left almost naked and in poor health.

When I was at last set free, I had the good fortune to come across a friend whom I had helped in a few amorous affairs, who, when he saw me in such a state, took pity on me and proposed that I assist him at the gaming houses as his croupier at the rate of two pesos a day.

I saw the clouds open up, for I knew how excellent this arrangement was; I would have done it even if he had only offered me two *reales*, for if the croupier isn't stupid, he can win as much as he likes, and I did just that. Day in and day out, my salary never fell below ten pesos, for, with the greatest grace in the world, I would pretend to be preparing my chewing tobacco, or blowing my nose, or taking out my watch, and in each of these maneuvers I would pilfer a peso or two. And that is how I got to live like a marquess; I put on princely airs, and there was not a scribe, office worker, or soldier who did not envy my lot. If in the days of my bonanza I had not gambled, I would be singing a different tune at this moment; but half the money I spent, and the other half I lost.

Nonetheless, my happiness would have lasted yet if my abilities had not caught the attention of my boss's weaselly barber, who, justifiably envious, informed on me. At the beginning, so I am told, my boss did not believe it; but on further insistence of that damn toady, he went to the gaming house, and, without my knowing it, witnessed my abilities for himself. When the game of *monte* ended, he brought me to his house; he locked us both in, made me take off my clothes, and twenty pesos fell from my clothing, for that night the devil had tempted me and I had overstepped the mark. I could not deny my stunt, and he broke his cane on my ribs and threw me out on the street in my underclothes, for that great miser even kept my clothes. Because he was not a gentleman, he did not know how to respect those of us who are from birth, and for this reason he treated me as one would a commoner and as if I had committed some crime in executing my necessary maneuvers.

In sum, I left the house half-naked and with my ribs nearly crushed. I crossed paths with a group patrolling the street; they closed in on me, and, seeing me dressed as I was, they took me for a thief and resolved to tie me up. But, as a man of talent always avails himself of this, especially in adverse times, I did not become alarmed. On the contrary, I made use of the patrol, and, adopting that tone of serenity that accompanies innocence, I said to the *alcalde*:[63]

"This was the only thing missing for the devil to take me away once and for all. Do you think a gentleman such as I should be branded a thief because he is naked, without anyone taking note that this is a shirt made of cambric linen and that this underwear is made of smooth Brittany linen, fabrics that thieves—at least the common purse snatchers—are little known to wear? I think it would be best if you and your patrol accompanied me home, where I would like to rest and heal from the damage done by the true thieves, who have left me in the state in which you see me."

---

[63] *Alcalde* is the word for mayor or government authority.

The *alcalde* and all his fellows felt pity for my misfortune; one of them lent me a cape, and all of them led me to my house.

When the landlady opened the door, I thanked the patrol. They bid me farewell, and I went upstairs to lie down and to cure myself with *aguardiente*.

The next day I could not get up, so the poor old landlady brought me a concoction made from I know not what ingredients, and with its help I started to improve by degrees until I could stand up and go out to the street. However, I no longer wanted to go to the gaming house, for I feared there wasn't a soul left who had not heard about the incident. If I had been recovering from lance wounds, I would not have refrained from seeing my friends, for marks from a lance do not embarrass a gentleman, but those from a common beating do.

In short, having recovered from the thrashing, and with my shame lessening over time, my only lamentation was that I was once again down to one outfit—although it was not a bad one—for in order to heal, eat, and pay for my room, I had been obliged to sell some things, pawn others, and lose them all. But now I was left with nothing, and I had to eat, and so it was that I went to take refuge once more in my warren—that is, the cafés, wine shops, and underground gaming and pool houses—where I searched for my friends and relatives, who helped alleviate my suffering for a few days.

On one of these days I had an encounter with a vile, wretched old man, and only by a hair's breadth did I escape downfall, as he who reads on will see.

Chapter 8

Relates the dispute he had with an old man about the Catrines, and the quarrel that ensued

To avoid lengthy prologues: I was in a café one day, waiting for some charitable acquaintance to offer to buy me lunch, and in truth I was very eager, for I had not had a bite to eat the day before; but alas!, my unlucky star resolved that none of my friends should appear.

I had made up my mind to leave when in walked a priest, accompanied by an old man of about sixty years of age. They took a seat at my table and greeted me courteously, and I returned their greeting in kind; they ordered lunch be brought, extended me an invitation, I accepted, and we ate merrily.

Over dessert they spoke about the debauched customs of the times. "I have heard," said the priest, "that these Catrines have a lot to do with the deterioration that we see."

"It cannot be the Catrines, my father," I exclaimed, "for the Catrines are good men, decent men, and above all they are nobles and gentlemen. They honor society with their presence, enliven tables with their conversation, amuse *tertulias* with their grace, edify young ladies with their doctrine, instruct idiots with their erudition, uphold the eminence of their ancestors with their conduct, cause the misers' money to circulate with their ingenuity, and increase the population as best they can; and, what is more, wherever they happen to be there is no sorrow, superstition, or fanaticism in sight, for they are fearless, cheerful, and they keep up with the times.

"In the eyes of a true Catrín nothing is criminal, nothing scandalous, nothing blameworthy; and truly, my father, you must realize how comprehensively our society benefits from this respectable, cheerful, lively, wise, and not a bit scrupulous youth (even more so if he is fine-looking). He does not marvel at the trap set by Peter, the covetousness of John, the deceitfulness of Mark Antony, or at anything on this earth.

"Ever filled with love for his fellow man, he forgives all, and he even tries to understand their way of thinking.

He defends the thief by pointing to his necessity; the co-quette, by blaming human misery; where the slanderer is concerned, the Catrín will say it is just his wit, the drunk, his joy, the rabble-rouser, his valor; and he even protects the heretic, citing the difference of opinions that every day is applauded and scorned. Thus, the true Catrín, he who depends on this noble race, is neither self-interested enough to lead a miserable life in exchange for heaven, nor cowardly enough to deny himself a good life in fear of a hell that he has not seen; accordingly, he follows the maxims of his comrades and satisfies his passions as it pleases him, or as he can manage, without becoming frightened by friars' sermons—for he takes care never to hear them—nor by the sad books that he does not read.

"In this way, the Catrín makes of himself a pleasant fellow wherever he goes. The girls value him highly, the young men respect him, the old fear him, and the hypo-crites flee from him. Now you see, my father, the useful-ness of these gentlemen the Catrines, of whom you have such a poor opinion."

I concluded my harangue, which seemed to me di-vine, and its incontestable argument. The priest shook his head as if to say no and, shooting me a furious look, took his hat and was about to rise from the table when that old dog of a companion took his arm, made him sit down, and said:

"Compadre,[64] I have been waiting a long time for an opportunity like this to disabuse you of the error you commit in believing that every cheerful, merry youth, every youngster dressed according to the style of the day, is a Catrín. No sir; not everyone is what they seem to be, nor does everyone seem to be what they are. The habit does not make the monk. As you can see, I am an old man, but not a senseless one. Anyone may dress himself according to his taste and proportions; nevertheless, a man's dress makes him neither a gentleman nor a rogue.

"There are many flashy youths who are glued to the fashion of the day, and for all this they are not Catrines, and there are others—down-and-out, everyday men without a cent—who are legitimate Catrines. Learn to distinguish between them and you will neither flatter nor offend someone who does not deserve it.

"Customs, compadre, conduct is the only measure by which we should evaluate and judge men. I would be willing to bet a bottle of wine that this gentleman is a legitimate Catrín and that he takes pride in this."

"It is true," I said, "and I do not regret having descended from such noble lineage."

---

[64] A form of address between a parent and the godfather of the child. More widely, this form of address is frequently used to express affection, social parity, or sympathy. The feminine equivalent, *comadre*, is used the same way.

"My little friend," answered the old man, "true nobility consists in virtue, and the superficial kind in money. How many thousands do you have?"

"I, none."

"Oh!, then you can quit all that talk about your nobility! You have neither the virtue to prove it nor the pesos to fake it; but let us get to the point.

"Compadre, you have just met a true Catrín, you have heard his erudition, and you have learned his system of conduct; and you will now see that you were misguided when you thought that all who dressed in the modern way were Catrines. But that is not all, friend; hear what the Catrines are like, beginning with their daily routine:

"The Catrín rises between eight and nine; from this hour until noon he goes to the cafés to see whether he might chance upon an acquaintance who will pay for his breakfast, lunch, or dinner. From noon until three in the afternoon he goes to the gaming house to see how he might wangle something, even if it is just a *peseta*.[65] If he does, he is satisfied, and giving thanks to his lucky saints, he returns to the cafés. From there, with his belly full or empty, he goes back to gaming just as diligently. If one

---

[65] The *peseta*, which is the diminutive form of the word *peso*, was worth a quarter of a peso, or two *reales*, in colonial Mexico (Frye xxxix).

of his *pesetas* "climbs," marvelous, and if not, he resumes his most honest of labors to get through the next day.

"As these devices can only provide for the most basic necessities at best, and because being a Catrín can be summed up as looking half-decent, dancing a waltz, and being an adulator, peacock, and fool, they draw upon these abilities to scam one man, swindle another, and dupe anyone they can. In this manner does Saint Parián tidy their faces to delude the fools or provide them clothes with which they trick those who believe that anyone who dresses with a certain amount of decency is a good man. But, after all, the Catrín is an inscrutable paradox, for he is a gentleman without honor, a rich man without an income, a beggar without an empty belly, a lover without a sweetheart, a brave man without an opponent, a wise man without books, a Christian without religion, and a scoundrel by anyone's measure."

Unable to suffer such a slanderous definition of our class, I shot a good number of profanities at the impudent old man. He reciprocated with a number of others. I tried to smash a chair over his head; the priest put himself in between us (as if I were one of those crackpots who fear priests and friars). Angered, I threw the chair at the old man but hit the priest; the latter became irritated, found a cudgel at hand, and hit me over the head. I became a vision of fury upon seeing my noble blood spilled by a few dead hands, and I jumped up to snatch a saber from someone who was nearby; but at that point everyone ganged up against me, calling me impudent and sacrilegious and threatening to end my existence if I did not contain myself. Seeing myself surrounded by so many idiots, I gave up and sat down where I was, and with that, the quarrel was ended.

Some advised me to apologize to the priest, for I had insulted him in public and without reason; but I paid no attention, knowing very well that a gentleman Catrín must never prostitute himself by begging anyone's pardon.

And so, everyone left, I did the same, and for some time I continued to suffer unendurable hardships and came to envy some acquaintances and friends who were doing better than I.

Some nights when I lay down to sleep I would hear a certain noise in my heart that scared me. On one of these occasions, I seemed to see standing next to my filthy bed the venerable priest from Jalatlaco, my dear uncle and undying preacher, who, gazing upon me with pitying eyes, and now and then a threatening stare, said to me:

"Pitiable youth, when will you wake up from this criminal lethargy? There can be no nobility where there is no virtue, nor admiration where good conduct is absent.

"You are twenty-eight years old, and each of these years has been poorly employed in the profession of vice.

Useless to yourself and harmful to the society in which you live because of your ghastly customs, you have aspired relentlessly to subsist with luxuries and comfort without doing any work or being useful in any way. Unhappy fool!, do you not know that as punishment for his sin man is born compelled to live from the sweat of his brow?[66] Do you not understand that just as one must not muzzle an ox when it treads out the grain[67] —in the words of the Spirit of truth[68]—Saint Paul wrote that he who does not work shall not eat?[69]

"It is true that you and many other lazy and immoral men like you manage without working to eat at the expense of others, but to what do you not subject yourselves? What afflictions do you not suffer? And finally, how does it end for all of you? You have already experienced hunger, nakedness, shame, beatings, jail, and illness. Woe unto you if you do not amend yourself! You have much to suffer yet, and your punishment will not be restricted to the present age, for as your life is

---

[66] Genesis 3.19: "By the sweat of your brow you will eat your food until you return to the ground, since from it you were taken; for dust you are and to dust you will return."

[67] Deuteronomy 25.4: "Do not muzzle an ox while it is treading out the grain."

[68] The Holy Spirit is referred to in this way in John 16.13: "But when he, the Spirit of truth, comes, he will guide you into all truth."

[69] 2 Thessalonians 3.10: "If a man will not work, he shall not eat."

disastrous, your death can be no other way. Take heed, and if you do not believe these warnings, this screaming of your conscience, prepare to reap the rewards of your scandalous behavior in hell."

Frightened by such a vision, the next day I went to discuss my troubles with a friend of great talent and well-ordered conduct, in the same manner as mine. Upon hearing me, my friend fell over with laughter and consoled me with the wholesome advice that you will read in the chapter that follows.

CHAPTER 9

CATRÍN LISTENS TO AND TAKES WICKED ADVICE
FROM A FRIEND; HE BECOMES A GREATER
LIBERTINE AND IS THROWN OUT OF THE COUNT
OF TEBAS'S HOUSE WITH HOT WATER

"It's easy to see you're a fool, Catrín," my good friend said to me. "Yes, you're a believer of visions, a novice, and a greenhorn of our great and respected order. My word, don't let them hear you calling yourself a Catrín or claiming to be worldly in the least! I have good reason, yes, good reason to be horrified at the sight of a young buck who's been a college student, a soldier, a gamer, and a rogue who is scared to death over a matter that any man of a strong and enlightened spirit like ours should laugh at.

"That rancid, senile uncle of yours wore you thin with sermons, and now you think that he is casting them at you after death. You're a blinkard and you frighten like a child with the boogeyman; but cheer up, pal, relax; shake off those visions of fear. Understand that the dead do not speak and that it's only in your unhappy imagination, agitated by your poverty, that these paper ghosts take form.

"Look, Catrín: our life is no more than a game, our existence short and frequented by misfortune, and there's neither rest nor happiness beyond its completion. No dead man has ever returned to earth to bring us proof of immortality; we've come from nothing and we'll return to nothing; our body will turn into ash and our spirit will be lost in the air; our life will pass like a cloud and disappear like mist, evaporated by the sun's rays. Our name will be erased from the memory of man and no one will remember our deeds. Let us savor every pleasure that is within our power; let us serve ourselves the most delicate wine, breathe the aroma of perfumes, crown ourselves with roses before they wither, may there be no pleasant object free from our lust, and let us leave traces of our gaiety in every corner; let us oppress the poor man, ruin the widow, disregard the gray locks of the old; may our forceful strength be the benchmark

of our justice; let us pay no heed to the holy days dedicated to the Lord; and above all let us exterminate the
just man, whose sight we cannot stomach."

"Those are big words," I told him. "Don't you see that
by following those maxims we'll make ourselves loathsome to the whole world?"

"How thick you are, Catrín, how primitive!" he replied. "It's true we'll be detested, but by whom? By four
of those crackpot hypocrites who call themselves pious.
But on the other hand, we'll be loved by all our male
companions and also our female companions the Catri-
nas, young, useful, lively people of liberal souls.

"You're a poor apprentice of true Catrinage, that
much is clear, and that's why you are shocked by everything, but would things be different for you if you
memorized and practiced the famous commandments of
Machiavelli?[70] In those times[71] you either plugged your
ears or set out to become a consummate politician. Since

---

[70] Nicolò Machiavelli (1469–1527) was an official of the Florentine
government who is remembered primarily for his work *The Prince*, a
political treatise that outlines how a successful ruler should conduct
himself. The concept that the ends justify the means, which runs
through much of the treatise, led to the origin of the term *Machiavellian*, defined as being "marked by cunning, duplicity, or bad faith"
("Machiavellian").

[71] Don Catrín presumably refers to the political environment of Machiavelli's Florence, where rivals made use of ruthlessness and cunning
in order to gain and safeguard power.

I began to observe them, I've lived the good life, I have many friends, and I'm met with displays of appreciation everywhere I go. It seems to me you're foaming at the mouth to learn them; for the sake of your happiness and advantage, listen:

MACHIAVELLI'S DECALOGUE[72]

1. Treat everyone pleasantly, but love no one.
2. Be very liberal in granting honors and titles, and flatter everyone.
3. If you manage to land a good position, serve only the powerful.
4. Howl with the wolves. That is, assume the character that works to your best advantage, even if it is most criminal.
5. If you hear someone lie in your favor, confirm his lie with a nod.
6. If you have done something that you do not wish to acknowledge, deny it.
7. Etch all injuries done unto you in stone, and any kindnesses in dust.

---

[72] The decalogue is spuriously attributed to Machiavelli in the novel. As Raúl Marrero-Fente notes, the author, whom we later realize is Don Cándido, continues his apocryphal game by suggesting that Albertus Magnus, a medieval theologian, mentioned this decalogue in one of his works, a clear anachronism, since Saint Albertus lived centuries before Machiavelli (112–13).

8. If you deceive someone, deceive him to the very end, for you have no need of his friendship.

9. Promise much and do little.

10. Be your own fellow man, and do not concern yourself with others.

"What do you think? Have these precepts surprised you?"

"Not much," I answered him, "for while they may be shocking when they are spoken, when they are practiced, they disguise themselves. As for me, I observe most of them carefully, and I know that nearly all our companions obey them to the letter. But now that I think of it, I recall that when I was a college student, I entered my professor's bedchamber one night, and as I was leaving his room I saw the same decalogue in Latin in a quarto book that was open atop his desk, and I don't know which saintly priest said at the end: *Si vis ad infernum ingredi, serva haec mandata*: If you want to go to hell, observe these commandments. That is the part that I do not much like."*

"And still you persist in your fanaticism," he answered me. "Pinhead: where have you seen the hell or the devils

* Niccolò Machiavelli, astute writer from Florence, and afterwards a false politician of France, wrote to his sectarians this evil decalogue, which Albertus Magnus had in the preface of his work entitled *Bonus politicus*, et cetera.

that make you believe so tenaciously? Carry out these precepts, follow my maxims, and you'll see how your luck changes. Suppose, yes, for the sake of argument, that there were such an eternity, such a hell; what is there to lose, then, if at the end of it all the devil takes you? Do you think you'd be the first person to be condemned? In that case, now that we shall all be condemned, let it be by our own choice; and if the devil takes us, let's do it right and, as they say, go out on a high note—that is, reveling, living it up, and having ourselves a merry life. Could there be any greater satisfaction than entering hell polished, fresh, rich, singing, dancing, and surrounded by ten or twelve young women? So, come on, Catrín, follow my advice and laugh at everything like I do."

Who could not but succumb to such solid reasons? Naturally, I gave many thanks to my wise friend and proposed to comply with his wholesome advice, and in accordance with my resolution, on that day I began to observe the decalogue with absolute precision, especially the fourth precept, learning to gain the favor of all those who could be of use to me; and thus, in a few days I was a Christian with the Christians; a Calvinist, Lutheran, Arian, etc. with the people of these denominations; a thief with the thieves; a drunk with the drunkards; godless with the unbelieving; and charming with all.

As you may well suppose, my beloved Catrines and companions, with this manner of conduct I reaped many friends, whose pockets provided me many good times, as well as some rotten ones, for just as I drank and ate and lived for free at times, at others I was beaten, in jail, or on the run, without having been directly responsible for the scuffles or deserving imprisonment; rather, it was my friends' fault. As you can imagine, I entertained all their whims, be these just or unjust, and for that, their enemies beat me for being their companion, and the judges punished me as an accomplice.

If I were to relate the details of all the adventures of my life to you, it goes without saying that it would hold your attention; but I have proposed to limit myself to just one tome, and so it is necessary to be brief, and to limit myself to the most memorable periods.

As I grew more enlightened through the lessons of my friend and mentor, and as I resolved to speak on any subject no matter how abstruse, one night I went with my friend to the Count of Tebas's house (for the Catrines are so noble that they fit in any home). After the *tertulia* there, everyone turned to the *merienda*;[73] having conversed about various matters, the conversation turned to the truth of the Catholic religion.

---

[73] A light meal served around midday.

All the attendees were fanatics; there was not a *spirit* with greater *strength* than mine. They spoke with great respect about dogma, the revelation, and tradition, and at the end, they concluded by saying that the enlightenment of this age consisted in libertinage, the consequences of which were the corruption of manners and the denial of the firmest truths.

"Speaking on the subject," said a chaplain, "there is a class of Catrines—that is, young people, perhaps highborn and respectable in dress but unproductive and lazy, ignorant, immoral, and *fachenda*, full of vice, who, not content with being rogues, would like everyone else to be like they are."

No sooner did I hear mention of the Catrines de Fachendas, whose surname I have had the happiness of inheriting, than I turned to defend their honor, saying:

"My dear father, temper your words: the Catrines are noble, Christian, genteel, and learned; they are very knowledgeable; many fanatics blame them without cause. What evil does a Catrín commit by dressing elegantly, as they say, by not working like a plebeian, by gambling his money and that of his pal, by seducing as many women as he can, by surviving by sponging off others, by living large, having fun, and living in the cafés, *tertulias*, and pool halls? Has this not been done by a thousand others, whether they had the honor of being Catrines or not?

"Now, why must they be designated fiendish and ungodly just because they do not practice confession, respect priests or churches, or kneel during the viaticum or mass, because they touch their hats neither during the Angelus nor for other such frivolities?

"If it is rumored that their education is inadequate, this is slander or unabashed envy. To confirm this, one need only watch a Catrín pass a piece of silverware to a lady, dance a few *boleras*[74] or a waltz, venture a risky bet, play a game of *tresillo*,[75] comb his hair and spruce himself up, speak with temerity and audacity about everything under the sun, and do other things that I do not mention because you would not believe me. Their utility is well known in the courthouses, cafés, taverns, pool halls, doorways, and promenades. Therefore, you should not speak ill of the Catrines, for they are more enlightened and useful than most others."

"You have left me without anything else to say, my little friend," said the chaplain. "You have just confessed, effortlessly and all on your own, who the Catrines are, what their occupation is, how remarkable their education

---

[74] *Boleras* or *boleros* were popular musical compositions that developed in late-seventeenth-century Spain and that could be sung or danced.

[75] A three-player card game.

is, and how worthy of public esteem the fruits of their labor are."

"As far as I am concerned," added the count, "I would appreciate it if you never set foot in my house again. I regret very much that you have paid me this one visit, and that you have revealed who you are so frankly. No, I do not wish for such a gentleman to honor my table, or such a teacher to instruct me, or a Catholic with such qualifications to edify me; and, so then, the *merienda* has concluded, take your hat and leave us in peace."

As soon as they heard the count express himself in this manner, all the attendees, perhaps hoping to please him, proceeded to mistreat me, even the servants; pushing and shoving, they expelled me from the living room, and a damn lackey nearly sent me rolling down the stairs; and, not content with subjecting me to these insults and humiliations, and disregarding the loftiness of my lineage, when I finally reached the street they threw a pot of boiling water on me, and you can imagine how I felt in that instant.

I wanted to go back and make them pay for this gross injury; but, seeing as I was alone (for my friend deserted me and sided with the count) and that everyone was angry, I contained myself. I thought prudently and took my leave, badly bathed and swearing on my word as a gentleman to avenge myself as soon as I had the means.

I arrived at my room, slept as I was wont, dried my clothes the next day, and arose wondering where and how I would get by. That day was, by the way, July 25.[76]

I came across a friend who took me to the festival of Santiago accompanied by a girl who was not bad to look at, and something came to pass during our lunch there that you will learn about in the next chapter.

Chapter 10

Which is full of adventures

God deliver us from any evil, as old women say. We were having lunch with the lovely girl, when all of a sudden there appeared a man with a saber in his hand, seething with rage, who, with a voice as terrible as the lightning's thunder, said:

"I had to see this for myself," and as he said this he began to slash and jab so many times that the three of us were not enough for all the blows. The woman fell to the ground with the first blow; my companion resorted to defending himself with a dagger. Lacking a weapon,

---

[76] In the Catholic calendar of saints, 25 July is dedicated to Saint James, or *Santiago* in Spanish.

I grabbed a plate of *mole*[77] and poured it over the brave man's head; he became angrier than he had been at the start, and he slashed at me with such precision and intention that he nearly put me in another place—that is, in my grave; but it knocked me out and left me with my head like a pomegranate.

When I awoke in the hospital, I learned that the man who had done such a thorough job on me was none other than the husband of the harlot whom my friend had brought along, that my friend went to jail, she was sent to a house of correction, the husband was left to wander freely, and I was taken to the hospital as a prisoner.

While I was there, God only knows what I endured with the surgeons, surgical assistants, and nurses; I can swear they did me more harm with their treatment than the jealous husband did with his pummeling. It was clear that they did it out of charity.*

At last I was pronounced healthy, although I was not convinced of this, considering how I felt; but like it or not, it was necessary to leave the hospital and go to jail,

---

* Here it is convenient to recall the barber and the madman.

---

[77] A thick, typically dark sauce that has pre-Hispanic origins. There are many varieties of *mole*, but common ingredients include chilies, tomatoes, seeds, many spices, and sometimes raw cocoa.

where a thousand testimonies were raised against me, for the least harmful of the things the husband said of me was that I was his wife's pim . . . pimpernel, or something like that.[78]

The notary wanted money to defend me; I hadn't a single *real*, nor did my friend, owing to which the whole thing was delayed a month or so; however, as they say, God smiles only upon those who already have the advantage, and at the husband's insistence the process continued and it was ruled that the woman should be sent to the Convent of Saint Lucas[79] for four years at her expense, our mutual friend to a penitentiary, and I to the street, under firm instructions never again to embroil myself in problems that were none of my business.

Fortunately, I escaped being sent to the clink; I went to my house, or the little portion of the house that was mine, and I found myself poorer—to such an extent that I did not have enough to maintain the appearance and decency of a Catrín.

---

[78] In the source text, Don Catrín writes that the husband accused him of being his wife's "al . . . calde," with "al . . . ca" almost becoming the word *alcahuete*, a go-between or pimp. *Alcalde* is the word for mayor or government authority.

[79] The Convent of Saint Lucas in Mexico was a house of confinement for wayward women, sometimes committed there by disapproving parents. Such institutions were referred to familiarly as *casas de recogidas* (women's reform houses) or *casas de Magdalenas* (Magdalene houses).

I had been down-and-out before this, I cannot deny it: every day, I had been obliged to spread black shoeshine on my boots and buff them with egg white, lemon, or onion; then there had been my little tailcoat, which I had had to give a thousand caresses with a comb; my shirt had required constant washing, hanging, and ironing with a mamey[80] seed. I had once owned a pair of polka-dotted pants, but these dots were the result of my curious manner of mending holes. I had owned a chain that hung from a buckle, which gave me the appearance of having a watch; a strip of muslin that, when given a nice washing, passed as an elegant handkerchief; a waistcoat swathed by so many contiguous patches that it formed a mosaic worthy of the most inspired artist; a cane that, though it was quite ordinary, I operated so well that it resembled a fine liana[81] cane from China; a hat of such a polite nature that it used to tip itself to passersby, but to which, using a mixture of glue, I gave such a haughtiness that it would not bow to the greatest monarch on earth, for it was stiffer than a poor man recently come into money. Finally, I had owned gloves—they were old, of course,

---

[80] An edible fruit that grows on trees and that contains a large, smooth seed. Mamey trees are indigenous to Cuba, parts of Central America, and Mexico.

[81] A vine-like plant that grows in tropical rain forests and temperate forests. It is characterized by long, woody stems.

but they covered my hands—a monocle, combs, brushes, creams, a looking glass, powders, a toothbrush, and other such charms, but when I got out of jail, as I had sold everything in order to eat, I had nothing.

And there you have me, my beloved Catrines, reduced to dire poverty. Dress shirts and superfluous things were alien to me, and eating for free required dressing elegantly, so how would it go for me? One tailcoat and one pair of pants that I was not able to pawn or sell were all that remained in the trunk that had once housed so many luxuries. But, taking that bit of fabric—how wondrous is the wise man's resourcefulness!—I gave it so many thousands of stitches, so many dyes and washes, that the most seasoned hawker would have sworn it was new. My old boots, thanks to the iron and the egg white, were left as lustrous *sicut erant in principio*,[82] as were the hat and waistcoat; with regard to a shirt, however, there was nothing I had that could stand in for one.

I had to eat the next day, and in order to eat it was necessary to go out and look for some friends; I was prepared to do anything, but my lack of a shirt filled me with consternation.

During this time of affliction, I remembered that I had owned a single shirt at one time, and that I had dubbed it

---

[82] "As they were in the beginning."

"singleshirt."[83] It was so far gone that all that was left of it was the collar and the flounces connected to a bit of fabric; but making a virtue of necessity, I cut and composed it as I could. The night was spent doing this and other things. The next day I was still in my underclothes ironing my flounces, when my landlord decided to visit, and he entered with little effort, for, as I had sold the key and had no way of keeping the door closed except with my little cane, which was very weak, it yielded upon the first thrust from my execrable landlord; the vile loiter-sack entered and found me half-naked, ironing my bit of cloth on a *petate*; he demanded payment with the imperiousness of a landlord owed five pesos and two *reales* in outstanding rent; he took inventory of my furnishings with one look; he demanded his rent money with resolution; I showed him my letters patent of nobility and told him that people do not demand payment in that way from gentlemen of my class, and that he was a churlish, insolent rogue. He became irritated at this and told me to shake my letters patent to see if any coins were in there, that paying was fair, that he would have none of my charlatanry, that I either give him his money or move

---

[83] In the original Spanish text, Don Catrín creates a pun by dubbing his shirt "camisola," playing on the meaning of the word *sola*, which means "only" or "alone." *Camisola* is a close cognate of the English *camisole*.

out that instant, and that in the very best of scenarios he would permit me to get dressed, but that I would not be taking a single scrap, since everything he saw around me would not suffice to cover my debt.

"You are a plebeian," I said, "a peasant, a scullion, a lowbred commoner; my family tree, the coat of arms of my house, my letters patent of *hidalgo* nobility, and the feats of my forebears that you see in these papers are worth more than you and all the houses of the nuns."

"That is all very well," responded the landlord. "You may be very genteel and very noble, and you may have infinite documentation of your grandeur, but the nuns eat neither letters patent of nobility nor titles: the rent must be paid or you move."

We went back and forth for a little while: I tried to catch hold of an old chair to break it once and for all over his head, but he seized another one nearby and we gave each other a thrashing of great scale, until finally the landlady came in and stopped us; but in the end the iniquitous landlord got what he wanted, which was to catapult me from the house, keeping my chest and my *memela*; nevertheless, he let me get dressed, which for folk of his class was veritable heroism; what luck I have, for even this was almost denied me.

When I took my leave I was somewhat embarrassed, but also very angry and sad, and in this state, with my papers tucked beneath my arm, I went in search of a friend. I found a lay brother who took pity on me and took me to his house, which he rented.

I was there for a few days; he had a pretty sister. I liked her, I made an advance, and she acquiesced. We became friends, and the lay brother found out. He spied on us, caught us, and made such good work of cudgeling me that I visited the hospital once again.

The judges ruled in his favor—such is the fate of good men such as I!—and when I was freed, I left the hospital naked.

I could not present myself to my friends this time, and so I solicited the patronage of women. A goodly old woman took me in; she lived in a small room attached to another house, and in her charge were five ladies, who negotiated the terms of their subsistence in the doorway. I had to see this without saying a word in order to eat, and I also had to procure the duck, *aguardiente*, coffee, and other things the men wanted.

This depravity could not but displease a gentleman of honor such as I, and thus, I determined to change my livelihood.

I took stock of my talents and weighed them against the decalogue that I had learned, and I came to the conclusion that I must seek out my comfort at the cost of the rest of the world.

In keeping with these principles, on a night when all the women were asleep, I bundled their clothing and cleared out.

The next day, before they came looking for them, I sold all the women's garments at the Baratillo,[84] stocked up on necessities, and settled in a neighborhood far away from theirs.

I carried on as I normally did, and to my good fortune I found Catrines at every turn. I spent some days in this way, but before long I could not even find a post to hang myself.

In the midst of my unhappy situation I found a good friend who emboldened me, telling me I was pathetic for not even being able to keep one body afloat, and declaring that he recognized talents very typical of a comic in me, and that I should seek a position and that I would remember him.

As he had stroked my vanity, I took his advice; I went to the Coliseum and tried out for a position, and they gave me the role of stagehand.[85] I accepted with de-

---

[84] A market in the Plaza Mayor where new and used merchandise was sold. The Baratillo became associated with illegality since many of the objects for sale there had been stolen (Gonzalbo Aizpuru 18).

[85] In the Spanish text, *"mite o metemuertos."* In the theater, this was the person in charge of clearing stage props during scene changes.

light, in the hopes that there would be possibilities of advancement.

In no time at all I was playing the sweetheart to every female comic, and not just to them but to as many women as I could; my ability started to gain recognition, and I would have been the leading man if the ladies had permitted me, but I devoted myself so sincerely to their services that in five months they landed me in the hospital of San Andrés[86] . . . God have mercy, what luck! Ever did I find myself in jails and hospitals!

What did I suffer from in San Andrés? Let he who was there speak. I narrowly escaped joining the ranks of the eunuchs. I left a half man, and this only by a miracle; but I was thin as a rail, colorless, with only a thin blanket draped over my shoulder.

In the midst of this situation, I came across a man who had been a servant in my house. As soon as he saw me, he recognized me and said:

"God have mercy, young sir, what an unhappy situation you are in!"

"I have just gotten out of the hospital," I answered him, "and I am fortunate to be standing on my own two feet."

---

[86] The hospital was established in 1779 and was located on Tacuba Street. It was founded by Archbishop Alonso Núñez de Haro y Peralta, viceroy of colonial Mexico (Martínez Barbosa 19–20).

"I am sorry for your misfortunes! I take it you do not have employment."

"As you can imagine, I do not."

"If you would be interested in a job as a doorman, I know that they are looking for one at Count Tebas's house; they pay eight pesos and meals."

"It would not matter if they offered eight hundred, I was not born to be a doorman, and much less to serve Count Tebas, my very own dearest godfather who cleansed my brow with holy water."*

"Well, sir," proceeded the servant, "could you get a position in a little shop? You could earn at least five *reales* a day there."

"Shut up, fool, would a gentleman such as I reduce himself to the level of a cigarette seller?"

"Well, then find a position as a clerk."

"Even less likely; my penmanship is that of a rich man, and individuals of my standing have college graduates serve them as scribes."

"Well, then in a shop."

"In a shop? Blackening myself with carbon and smearing myself with animal fat?"

"Well, then . . ."

---

* See chapter 9, in which he was baptized like a chicken in boiling water.

"Enough of your *well, thens*. Have you forgotten that I am Sir Don Catrín de la Fachenda, noble, illustrious, and genteel through and through, as were the four grandparents from whom I sprang? How can you imagine a personage of my stature subjecting himself to serving anyone in this life, unless it were the king himself? Go, go, and do not add to my hardships with your cloddish ideas."

The servant became vexed and said to me:

"Well, Sir Don Catrín, keep your nobility and gentility, and keep your hunger and your shabby blanket."

Saying this he left, and I kept walking without knowing where to go.

It was three in the afternoon and I had not eaten so much as a crust of bread, nor did I have any hopes of doing so; I did not even know where I would take shelter that night. I had nothing left but half a shirt, a pair of pants, boots, a hat, and a blanket, all old, dirty, and gone to pot. In a similar state did I find my letters patent of nobility, which I had brought with me to the hospital and which I was carrying beneath my arm that day.

Starving as I was, I resolved to pawn these treasures for whatever I could get, albeit with great sorrow in my heart. I entered a shop and told the keeper my bold idea.

This individual saw the papers and then looked me in the face, filled with astonishment, and after a few moments, almost with tears in his eyes, said to me:

"Is it possible, Catrín, that it is really you, my godson, the adored son of my good friend? How could it be? If I did not see you with my own eyes, if I were not holding your baptismal certificate in my hands, I would believe that you were trying to fool me."

After the thousand questions that he asked me and the thousand lies that I told him regarding the provenance of my misfortune, he brought out one of his suits and twenty pesos, which he gave to me, and with this I took my leave very contentedly.

With this bit of succor, my stomach found relief, and I stocked up on things that I needed like a little cane, a watch chain, and other such necessary supplies. When night fell I took refuge at my old landlady's house, and as I still had twelve or fourteen pesos remaining, she received me with great hospitality. The next day I took a room, sent for my mattress and chest, and lo and behold, I was once again a man of respectability, rubbing elbows with my friends at the cafés.

As Lady Fortune had stung me before, I shuddered at the thought of falling again on miserable times, so I tried to prepare myself against her future assaults. With this intention, I went to discuss my troubles with a friend who was worse off than I but who had the talent, audacity, and disposition for anything, and he emboldened me to do that which you will read about further on.

Chapter 11

He accepts some bad advice and is sent
to the Morro Castle of Havana

Who could be so ungrateful and boorish as to deny the advantages afforded to us by the wholesome advice of friends? This friend of mine, to not mince words about the matter, persuaded me to help him steal five thousand pesos from an old merchant whom he believed slept alone.

Being well instructed in the precious decalogue, and understanding that necessity lies outside the jurisdiction of everyday laws, I took his advice. We settled on a day and time, went to the shop around eight o'clock at night, walked in to catch the owner unawares and, thinking that it was in our best interest, locked the door behind us; but in doing so we only doomed ourselves, for at the first yell from the old man, four armed youths emerged, put their pistols to our chests, tied us up, and took us to jail. We could not deny what our intentions had been, and on these grounds alone we were sentenced to two years' imprisonment at the Morro Castle of Havana, and we went to serve our time with great dismay.[87]

We were of great use in that city, for we repaired the Castle of the Point and the Castle of the Prince,[88] worked in the arsenals, cleaned in accordance with the regulations set by the authorities, and performed other such useful tasks.

Many were the episodes of hunger, nakedness, and fatigue that we suffered during that time; but the most unbearable part was the harsh, coarse, and even cruel treatment given to us by that cursed devil of an overseer, under whose command we worked. Needless to say, he was a mulatto, vile, crude, and unaccustomed to dealing with gentlemen of my class;[89] and so whenever it pleased him or whenever it seemed we were not working quickly

---

[87] The Morro Castle of Havana, or the *Castillo de los Tres Reyes del Morro*, is a colonial-era fortress located on top of a rocky promontory overlooking Havana Bay. King Philip II of Spain ordered construction of the Morro in the sixteenth century to protect Havana from the frequent attacks by pirates. It later served as a prison.

[88] The Castle of the Point, or the *Castillo de San Salvador de la Punta*, was another colonial fortress built during the reign of Philip II to protect the port of Havana. It is located a short distance from the Morro, on the other side of the bay. The Castle of the Prince, or the *Castillo del Príncipe*, was built for the same purposes in the eighteenth century.

[89] The narrator's blatantly racist representation of the overseer serves to undermine the notion—held by many at the time—that Europeans were superior to people of color or mixed race.

enough, he thrashed our ribs with his whip. This made me seethe, and I assure you that had it not been for the fact that I was unarmed and fastened to my dear companion by a chain like vowels in a diphthong, I would have taught that despicable churl how to behave around gentlemen of my rank.

Nonetheless, I sent a letter to the governor in which I complained of the abuses of that Carib,[90] citing my well-known nobility and presenting my letters patent and other papers. But, as fortune delights in harassing the illustrious and persecuting the innocent, not only did the governor refuse to give me justice, but he exasperated me with the following decree:

"Nobility is proven better with good conduct than with documents. Endure your hardships as best you can, for a thief is not noble and does not deserve to be treated any better."

What do you think of this, my dear companions? Was this not a flagrant injustice on the part of the governor? Of course it was, and I became so infuriated that I cursed every nobleman on earth; I tore up my papers, gnashed

---

[90] A term that refers to an indigenous people of the Lesser Antilles and parts of South America. From the sixteenth to the nineteenth century, it was often used synonymously with *cannibal* since some early Spanish accounts of the New World described cannibalistic practices among some of its people.

them with my teeth, and threw them as tiny pieces into the sea, for they were useless to me.

Two years finally passed, I regained my freedom and returned to Mexico, my homeland. But, as I had torn up my letters patent of nobility and renounced everything that smelled faintly of nobility, I applied myself wholly to having a good time and shamelessly getting by any way I could.

I degenerated from the illustrious family of the Catrines and joined the impure one of the common thieves. Whenever I had a scrap of a coat or frock coat, I associated with thieves of that attire, and when I did not, I would give my blanket an air of elegance and go with the people who wore these too, conforming my ideas, words, and actions to those of the people on whom I depended.

Among the benefits reaped as a result of my time in jail were three principal ones: losing all sense of shame, drinking in excess, and fighting over anything. These lessons made my life a little less difficult. My friends were just like me; my attire and my food, according to my means; my living quarters, wherever the night found me; my *tertulias*, the cafés, pool halls, wine shops, *pulquerías*,[91] and taverns.

---

[91] Establishments selling *pulque*, an inexpensive alcoholic beverage produced by fermenting the juice of the maguey plant.

In any event, for better or for worse, I was never without the comforts of food, drink, and freedom to roam, all without doing work of any kind, for the two years of work in Havana had left me so chafed that I solemnly swore and took a vow never to work at anything in this life, a vow I have upheld with the scrupulousness consistent with a conscience as righteous and pious as mine.

Despite the privations that persecute all learned, decent men such as I, every now and then fortune's happier side shone down on me. If during these times I managed to procure a reasonable gig, then I would dress elegantly and join my old friends, for as birds of a feather flock together, and as a leopard cannot change its spots, so I, who knows why,* gravitated toward Catrinage even after having forgotten my nobility.

But do not believe that fortune smiled upon me out of goodness or by chance, but rather because I conducted such active and honest enterprises as the one I will relate to you now.

One time, dressed as a Catrín and without half a *real* to my name, I came across a woman selling a string of pearls in the Parián, for which she asked eighty pesos. I

* The wellborn youth, even if he has not had a sound education or has not made good use of it, and even if he has prostituted himself unfortunately like our hero, remembers his birthplace from time to time and feels ashamed of his actions and wishes that he could go back to the place where he wandered off course.

offered to pay sixty-eight for the said necklace, and she agreed to the price. I then led her to a convent, explaining that my uncle, a government authority, wanted to see the pearls, for it was he who had sent me on the errand for my sister, his niece. The good woman believed me by virtue of my tailcoat and my little cane. She gave me the string of pearls and set off with me to the convent, where she remained awaiting her money at the entrance. Then, just like in the stories, I went in through the entrance and left through the false door. I bet that senseless woman is still waiting for me. That afternoon, I sold the string of pearls for thirty pesos to a relative in the army, who, when he heard of the bargain, and after I advised him not to try to sell it in Mexico, purchased it without asking for a guarantor or making any sort of fuss. Such were my wiles. And is this not proof of extraordinary talent, well-regulated conduct, and outstanding merit? Let the Catrines and the petty thieves respond.

In one of these moments of good luck, I was at a café when in walked poor Taravilla, my old friend, comrade-in-arms, and housemate, about whom I spoke to you in the third chapter. But alas, what a state the unhappy fellow was in! Dressed in the old uniform of a retired lieutenant, he held himself on two crutches, for he was completely lame.

"Catrín, friend, is that you?"

"Yes, friend," I replied. "What a miracle it is to see you! But what has happened to you? Did you lose the use of your limbs in some battle? You poor man, that must be it! Come sit and order whatever you would like."

He ordered what he wanted and then said to me:

"Oh, brother! It's Venus who has treated me this badly, not Mars. Five times has Mercury paid a visit to my bones, causing me to suffer terrible pains. I've sworn not to tempt the enemy again, but scarcely do I catch a glimpse when I forget my oath. I charge forward and always end up defeated. In one of these campaigns, when I was weak and badly injured, I was overcome and reduced to the ultimate misery; I was taken prisoner and made to exercise the humble profession of *picador*, and I was forced to take on two animals; my abilities were an inadequate match for their spirit, and in one of the falls that I took, they overpowered me and left me in the state in which you see me."[92]

He went on to relate his adventures to us—not only mentioning his accomplices but also their names, what they looked like, and the streets and houses where they lived—with such self-possession and grace that we all

---

[92] Extended metaphor describing a venereal disease through images of Venus, the goddess of love, and Mars, the god of war. The messenger god Mercury also refers to the highly toxic metal used in the painful treatment of syphilis. The term *picador*, a horse rider in a bullfight who tires the bull by jabbing it with a lance, is also a common sexual euphemism.

laughed and celebrated his sharp memory and wit. I tire-
lessly made fun of his lameness.

Who could have told me that in a few days I would
find myself in worse circumstances? That is how it went,
as you will all see in the following chapter.

Chapter 12

In which he relates how he lost
a leg and saw himself reduced to
the wretched state of beggar

Taravilla ate and drank on my tab that day, as I had done
with others; after all, he came from the illustrious race
of the Catrines.

He said goodbye, and after a little while we all left for
our houses or the house of someone else.

I spent a good amount of time alternating between a
petty thief and a Catrín, and owing to a certain amorous
adventure (of which I do not write for fear of offending
your chaste ears), on one occasion I fought with the husband of my damsel, and he had the good fortune of stab-
bing me viciously in the left thigh, nearly cutting it in
two with his knife.

People came at the sound of my shouting . . . how
heartless the people of Mexico are! . . . Could they be like

that everywhere in the world? Many gathered around us out of curiosity and watched us brawl, with no one trying to separate us; my enemy wounded me, dragged his wife away and hit her, and no one impeded it; he took her somewhere, and no one followed him; I lay there bleeding to death, and everyone looked at me and said: "Poor thing!" But they did not call for a confessor or a doctor, and no one even tried to stop the bleeding!

As more and more idiots assembled, the size of the crowd prompted a good official (for, among the countless bad ones, one inevitably finds a couple who are good and wise) to come over, and he called a patrol, which took me to the judge. The latter determined that I should be taken to the hospital. My statement was taken, I said whatever suited my fancy, and the outcome of it all was that they cut off my leg, for gangrene was setting in quickly.

They cut it off, in effect, and I narrowly escaped death in the process. Some days later they kicked me to the street, which I bore happily, for I had feared that I would have to answer for my actions in prison.

As I could not stand on one leg as cranes do, I had to come into a pair of crutches, which did not come without work on my part.

With these hulking contraptions and my clothing in tatters, I left, as I have said. But where was I to go? To God's streets to beg for money, for on one leg I was in no position to come up with a ruse, nor could I walk as lightly as I did when all my members were working correctly.

Although I had left all my shame in Havana and cared about nothing in the world, I confess that it was very difficult for me to be a beggar at first; but alas, it was either ask for alms or die of hunger.

At the beginning my new trade was very onerous, for I had no knack for humbling myself, insisting, or receiving insults patiently; but it was just a matter of time. In two months I was master of the panhandlers and the idlers.

Once I got a feel for the business and learned its immense and seldom-pondered advantages, I embraced it wholeheartedly. I said to my old cloak:

"A beggar I shall be *ex hoc nunc et usque in saeculum*."[93]

In keeping with this proposal, I devoted myself to studying relationships, familiarizing myself with pious houses and people, learning what saint's day it was, modulating my voice in such a way that my words caused compassion, and cultivating other equally valuable skills, which I came to master with such perfection that it brought me to the attention of others, and every person who heard me felt sorry for me.

"Poor little weakling," some said, "and so young!"

---

[93] "Now and forever."

I never had fewer than ten or twelve *reales* at the end of the day, in addition to the food that I was given and which was too much for me to finish, so much that I felt bad having it all to myself; and thus, I looked for a poor girl with whom to share my happiness and my treasure trove.

In effect, I found a girl named Marcela, of great poise and attraction, whom I supported with what little means I had. She looked after me with painstaking care, and she had so much grace and economy that in four months she dressed like a lady and dressed me up too. And so it was that each night, after collecting my alms, I went home, dressed myself up like a Catrín, put on my peg leg, and went to have a light meal with Marcela at a place where no one would recognize me.

I myself marveled to discover that what I could not accomplish as a college graduate, soldier, card sharp, Catrín, or petty thief, I could accomplish as a beggar. By this, I mean supporting a good girl and her servant in a three-room dwelling as decent as I, all without working at anything or incurring debts, but by living instead from the ardent piety of the faithful. Oh, sacred charity! Oh, blessed alms! Oh, rewards of light efforts! How many would follow your lead if they knew your advantages! How many would abandon their workshops! How many would accept all the risks and pay gold coins so that someone would scratch their eyes out, cut their legs off, and line them with sores and cysts in order to join our wasteful but well-supplied company and have a share of our spoils?

I lived the good life with my trade. I assure you, friends, that I did not envy the finest of professions, for I told myself that even in the most profitable one, a man had to do at least some work to have money, while in my trade one acquired money without working, which had been the goal to which I had aspired since I was a boy.

Having experienced for myself the advantages of this employment, I am no longer shocked by the great number of decent, healthy men and women and good-looking boys and even girls that exercise the laudable trade of beggar.

I am surprised even less by the great number of hypocrites speaking against them. Virtue is always persecuted, and happiness is ever envied. Stop, cruel and ill-intentioned writers, stop calling pitiable beggars the leeches of the societies that enable them. Don't tire yourselves trying to prove that it is poorly guided piety to give alms to a person begging in God's name without determining whether he is a layabout or a destitute soul in legitimate need. Stop hardening the hearts of others with your assurances that idlers who beg to feed their vices greatly outweigh the truly needy who turn to begging for survival.

We all know that your biting criticism is the result of nothing more than malice and well-worded envy. Fools! Won't you cease to turn pious hearts against us and instead enjoy the benefits we do with the same effortlessness? Are two crutches and a little basket so costly? Does it require so much talent to pretend to be blind, one-armed, or lame? Is it so bitterly painful to give oneself lesions and other such things? Need one study at the university to learn a thousand things, even if these can be quite complex and illogical? And lastly, need one endure any exams or do any favors to gain acceptance into our dirty, disgusting, and well-provisioned guild? Well, what are you waiting for, imbeciles? Come join us; abandon your pens, put on a gag, and supply yourselves with some filthy rags; do as we do and you will enjoy the same comforts and advantages.

That is how I would address our enemies, and if I had ten or twelve children of my own I would teach them this easy trade, send them to live in different cities, and assure them that if they lived with a bit of thrift, they would be set for life.

Delighted with my calling, which came to me like a gold coin surfacing in a muddy puddle, I lived very happily with my Marcela, who, as she was taken care of in every way, was crazy about me, and nothing that she could do could displease me. That time was filled with abundance, satisfaction, and pleasure. It is true that my life had its share of domestic episodes and scenes on the street. My imprudence mixed with *aguardiente* were to blame for this. But Marcela knew how to bring these to a happy conclusion: when I got into a state, she would shove me onto the bed and take my crutches, and there I would remain squawking like a parrot but unable to get off of the mattress or do her any harm. With this, she would sober me up promptly, give me four caresses, and we would be fast friends once again.[94]

Not so with the unpleasant episodes on the street, which were occasioned by the envy of my companions. These were down-and-out fellows like me, who, feeling that I was stealing bread from their mouths, never ceased to insult me among themselves and to my face:

"What a cursed weakling, that shifty, lazy bum! Why doesn't he go to a shop or get a post somewhere where he can be of some use, instead of staying around here, fat

---

[94] Don Catrín uses the term *chispa*, or "spark," to refer to his inebriation in the original text. Lizardi explains this term with the following note: "'To catch the spark' is one of the many phrases used here to mean to become drunk, and 'to shake off the spark' means to become sober."

and sated and without a scratch, pretending to be sicker than we are, and taking our livelihood from us with his damn mouth?"

That is how those poor men took it; but, making like I did not hear them, I persisted in my begging with greater force and continued collecting my crumbs. However, their envy bothered me.

For little more than a year I enjoyed the sweet satisfactions I have described; but, as everything in this world has an end, that of my good luck arrived, as you will see in the chapter that follows.

CHAPTER 13

IN WHICH HE RELATES THE END OF HIS
GOOD LUCK, AND THE REASON FOR THIS

Who could believe that luxuries and self-indulgence are oftentimes the killers of men? Strange as this may seem, it is an eternal, proven truth, especially for rich men.

The treatment that I gave to myself, with the exception of the rags I wore in the daytime, was equal to that of the most affluent, spoon-fed fellow. On a typical day I would rise from my bed around nine or ten o'clock in the morning, and this routine played a role in destroying my health.

I never learned the maxim of the Salernitana school[95] that says that seven hours of sleep are enough for the young man and the old. *Septem horas dormire sat est juvenique, senique.*

This, along with what Solomon says in his Proverbs about those who are lazy, was unknown to me.*

On the other hand, my table was abundant enough to feed three, and tempting to the extreme, for Marcela's mother had been a cook for a nobleman and for several rich people, and Marcela had perfected the art of charming the palate, provoking the appetite, and ravaging the stomach. Each day she would make me a thousand tasty and heavily seasoned morsels. These gifts were ruinous for me in the end.

At the time I did not know that the palate slays more men than does the sword, as a French writer once wrote,† or that Alexander, who emerged victoriously from a thousand battles, was bested by gluttony and sensual pleasures, and that he died at thirty-two years of

---

* "Do not be too fond of sleep, or you will fall upon scarcity. Be active and you will live in abundance. A little slumber, a little folding of the hands to rest, and poverty will come upon you like an armed man." Proverbs 24.

† Blanchard.

---

[95] One of the most important medical schools in medieval Europe. It was founded in the ninth century in Salerno, Italy.

age; that frugality extends life by the same amount that immoderation shortens it; that Galen,[96] an ancient physician who was very wise for his time, said: "When I see a table laden with a thousand delicacies, it seems to me that what I see are visions of colic, dropsy, incontinence, paroxysm, bouts of diarrhea, and every sort of ailment." The following words from the sage were unknown to me: "The excesses of the mouth have caused many a death, but the sober man will live a much longer time."

The wise Englishman John Owen[97] wrote an epigram about this in Latin, which I will translate for you:

> Few doctors
> and little medicine;
> Have little suffering,
> Sober cooking,
> If to live a long life
> You aspire.

"Moderation and work," says the Genevan philosopher (Rousseau), "are man's two best doctors: work excites his hunger, and moderation hinders him from abusing it."

---

[96] Claudius Galenus (129–216) was a Greek physician and philosopher whose ideas had a lasting influence on medical theory and practice in Europe.

[97] John Owen, a writer born in 1563 or 1564, was famous for his numerous Latin epigrams.

One physician asked Father Bourdaloue[98] what regimen he followed, and the wise man answered that he ate only one meal a day. "Do not make," responded the physician, "do not make your secret public, as you would bring an end to our profession, for we would have no one to cure."

Saint Charles Borromeo,[99] being very sick at the time and noting the contradictions among physicians concerning the nature of his illness, sent them away. He tempered his table, renounced treats, subjected himself to a simple and regular diet, and was cured and gained enough vigor to carry out the labors of his bishopric, to which he applied himself with such zeal.

The author of Ecclesiastes says: "If you are seated at a great table, let yourself not be brought to excess by the mouth's appetite." "Do not be," he says in another place, "among the last to rise from the table, and bless the Lord who has reared you and who has showered you with his gifts . . ."

I knew nothing of these things, whose observance leads, in effect, to health and vigor. The last friend that I had, and who I now think was the only one, taught me

---

[98] Louis Bourdaloue (1632–1704) was a French Jesuit priest.
[99] Charles Borromeo (1538–84) was an Italian cardinal and archbishop who played an important role in the Counter-Reformation in Italy.

these rules, but it was too late, for my energies were by then enervated, my health debilitated, and my spirits exhausted.

Among my killers, the greatest of all was the excessive use of liquors. I was careful not to get drunk during the day so as not to lose credit with my pious patrons; by night, however, I would get dead-drunk.

This abuse not only damaged my health but exposed me to a thousand jokes, slights, and brawls. I knew the source of my misfortune, but I did not have the fortitude necessary to abandon it.

One night (I was not yet very drunk), I was drinking with my nocturnal friends in a tavern, and I was drinking more than everyone. One of the guests took pity on me, I know not why, and with great subtlety he made it so that the conversation turned to the danger of drinking in excess. Oh, and what a wonderful preacher did we have! He said:

"Gentlemen, there is nothing to debate, everything that God created, he created for man, and it is true that a nice swig of wine or *aguardiente* revives our strength and aids digestion, invigorates the spirit and infuses happiness into our blood, and, distracting us from the cares and sorrows all around, grants us a tranquil and satisfying sleep.

"I myself am very fond of a glass of wine, especially when I am in the company of friends. I am not priggish in that way; I remember that God himself says through Ecclesiastes: 'Wine was created from the beginning to make man merry, not to make him drunk. Drunk in moderation it brings joy to the soul and heart, and drunk with temperance it brings health to the spirit and body. It is just as true that, drunk in excess, it brings bitterness to the soul and causes quarrels, indifference, and many evils.'*

"Along with the ravages it causes to the health and spirit, it disturbs man's reason and makes him an object of ridicule to all who observe his clumsy movements, slurred words, and befuddled speeches.

"When a man is so drunk that he is incapable of talking or moving, then he is deadened and can cause neither anger nor laughter. However, when he is half-boozed or half-drunk, as you all call it, this is when his idiocies cause laughter or irritation. Even distinguished men have been rendered ridiculous and scandalous, history reminds us, by no other cause than the large quantities that they drank.

"Who would not roar with laughter to hear that the famous poet Chapelle, drinking one night with a French

* Ecclesiastes 31, v. 35, et cetera.

134

marshal, resolved that they should both become martyrs, that they should go to Turkey and preach the Christian faith? 'There,' Chapelle said to the marshal, 'they will apprehend us and take us before some *bajá*;[100] I will answer with great resolve, and so will you, marshal, sir, and they will impale me and then impale you; then we will go straight to paradise.' The marshal became angry that the poet had put himself first, and such animosity grew between the two that they charged at each other, sending all the chairs, tables, and sideboards rolling. How great must have been the mirth of the people who gathered to calm them down when they learned the reason for their quarrel.

"Monsieur Blanchard was careful to preserve this anecdote for us, and it struck the said abbot as even more comical that another time, in the house of the famous Molière, this same Chapelle, after drinking with his companions, displeased by the miseries of life, convinced them that it would be an act of great heroism to kill oneself in order not to suffer. Convinced by the poet's words, his comrades resolved to go drown themselves in a river that was close to Molière's house. Then they went and threw themselves into the water. Some people from the

---

[100] In the Ottoman Empire, a senior official, viceroy, or governor; or, in certain Muslim countries, an honorific title.

house and others who were nearby got them out. The rescued men became angry and tried to kill their helpers for such an affront. The poor servants ran to take refuge in Molière's house. When he discovered the cause of the quarrel, he asked the men why, if they were his friends, had they wanted to exclude him from the glory they pursued with their project. Everyone agreed that he was right, and they invited him to go to the river in order to drown himself with them.

"'Let us take our time,' Molière replied, 'this is a great enterprise and it must be treated with maturity. Let us leave it for tomorrow, because if we drown ourselves at night, they will say that we were desperate or drunk. It would be better to do it during the day and in front of everyone, for that way our bravery will shine more splendidly.'

"The friends were convinced; they retired to bed, and the next day, the wine vapors having dissipated, they all decided to preserve their lives."

I was able to understand the windbag's stories up to this point; but, as I was drinking while he sermonized, I fell asleep on the table, and the tavern keeper had the kindness to lay me down on a bench.

At four o'clock in the morning I came to or awoke, and, alarmed to find myself in a nice cape or jacket, I arose, rubbed my hands together, washed my face, drank coffee, and, quite wrinkled and rumpled, went home to don my very finest in order to make a living, as usual.

My life remained like this for only a short time longer, for the dropsy that I suffer from as I write these lines began, setting in motion all the catastrophes that you will read about in the fourteenth chapter of this legitimate and true story.

Chapter 14

IN WHICH HE RELATES HIS ILLNESS AND THE
MISFORTUNES IT CAUSED, AND THE NARRATION OF OUR
FAMOUS DON CATRÍN IS COMPLETED BY SOMEONE ELSE

My dear ones: as I write this chapter, which I think will be the last one of my life, I feel quite anxious, my belly has become enlarged and my legs . . . I mean, my leg has swelled up more than I like, and for these reasons it is to be expected that this chapter will be less methodical, erudite, and elegant than the others from my admirable story, for, as you know, *conturbatis animus non est aptus ad exequendum munus suum*: the disordered spirit is unfit to fulfill its functions, according to Cicero or Antonio de Nebrija, from whom I must have read this saying. Praise, my friends, praise my erudition and modesty, which assert themselves even on the brink of death. Other writers cannot do as much in the very prime of youth; but let us dispense with overtures, let us continue the text, come what may.

Anasarca, or general dropsy, overpowered my precious body; it confined me to my house; it drove me to my bed. Marcela called the doctor, and between him and the pharmacist half of what I had saved was taken, and in the end they told me there was no hope.

My dear Marcela, once she heard that I was out of the game, moved away one night just like that, taking everything that was left with her, though she left me in the landlady's care, which was no small favor. On that same unfortunate day, the aforementioned landlady obtained a bed for me in the hospital, brought me to it, and there I was, without a *real* or any trinkets that amounted to it, abandoned by her whom I loved most, filled with sadness, and given over to the discretion of the doctors, quacks, and medical assistants of this blessed hospital where I find myself, and where I never imagined I would find myself on account of what I had saved up and the love Marcela professed for me.

But alas! Ungrateful, false, greedy women! Woe unto the man who falls for your honeyed words, oaths, affection, and promises. You love and adulate men as long as they can be of use to you, but hardly do you see them fall on hard times, abandoned, imprisoned, or bedridden when, forgetting their sacrifices and efforts, you desert them and consign them to oblivion.

Open your eyes, Catrines, friends, relatives, and comrades, open your eyes and do not trust these seductive sirens who pretend to love and who enslave their lovers in the process, do not trust these dogs who wag their tails and revel while they feed off your wealth.

There are many Marcelas, many lowly and greedy women in the world. Let the flatterers of the fairer sex say that there are respectable, loyal, and uninterested women; let them point out for me two or three from history; I will tell them that it could be true, that such women could exist, but I have never had the good fortune of meeting one of them; instead I had Marcela, a perfidious and ungrateful woman, who, as soon as she lost hope in my surviving, robbed me, left me without any means of getting by, and, as a grand token of her love, left me in the care of an old woman.

However, may God repay that old woman, for thanks to her piety I am still alive and able to write these few lines.

The dropsy, the water, the mucus, or what have you, which every day fattens me more and more, and I am troubled by such robustness . . .

I am writing this bit by bit, without order, and that is how you must read this.

The doctor tells me that I am dying and to prepare myself. Terrible report!

The chaplain has come to give me confession, and I, to get him off my back, have told him of four stories and fourteen tiny faults.

He absolved me and applied the bull of indulgence.[101]

They brought me the viaticum, and they performed a ceremony that was very strange to me, for in my life I have only confessed twice at most.

The intern, Don Cándido, has become a friend of mine; he pampers me and preaches to me, but sometimes he serves as my scribe. I trust him, and I have charged him with the task of finishing my story; he offered to do this; he is fanatical and will keep his word, even if he erases this comment. But he is a good man.

They must think that I am in very poor condition, for they have put a Christ figure at my feet; who knows what all those things mean: my spirit is very strong.

The intern admires my talent, sympathizes with my condition, and gives me advice.

He begins to tire me. He wants me to make a declaration of faith; repent my past life, as if it had not been

---

[101] In the Catholic Church, a formal document reducing the amount of penance one must complete in the atonement of sins.

excellent; ask forgiveness for the public disorder I have caused, as if such humility were appropriate in a gentleman of my class. He wants me to forgive those who have offended me, and that is for lowly people—avenging personal offenses is a point of honor, and there is no middle ground* between gaining satisfaction by redressing an insult and coming into disgrace by letting it go.

This friend of mine wants so many things that I cannot satisfy him in all of them. He wants me to make a general confession in my very last breaths. Have you heard of such nonsense?

He tries to frighten me at every turn with death, judgment, eternity, and hell. My spirit is not so weak as to quiver before these hobgoblins. Not once have I seen a damned soul, nor do I have evidence of the eternal rewards and punishments of which I am told. But if, to my great misfortune, they turn out to be true, if there is a Supreme Judge who repays men's acts according to the nature of these—that is, good acts with glory and bad acts with eternal suffering—then I have it coming to me, and if I somehow manage to get out of this one, it won't be by much.

---

* Those who think in this way do not know what real honor is made of.

Even when I have these thoughts, I do not cower, nor do I feel any strange emotion in my heart: my spirit enjoys a calmness and peacefulness that are imperturbable.*

My uneasiness agitates me greatly; my chest swells up like my belly . . . I'm suffocating . . . Intern, my friend, continue my work . . .[102]

CHAPTER 15

CONCLUSION. WRITTEN BY THE INTERN

No longer could the unfortunate Don Catrín continue dictating his story; the dissolution of his humors[103] reached its limit, his lungs became filled with cirrhoses, he could not breathe, and he died.

He was given the corresponding funeral rites, and, according to the hospital's statutes, his warm corpse was

---

* "The sinner's peace is terrible," says the Holy Spirit.

---

[102] At this point the reader realizes that Don Cándido is responsible not only for the final chapter but also for the author's notes throughout the narrative. While they may seem informative and didactic, the apocryphal notes in chapter 9 reveal Don Cándido as a complex figure, or, as Marrero-Fente has called him, "un espíritu voltairiano que se burla de todas las convenciones" ("a Voltairean spirit that makes fun of all conventions"; 113; my trans.).

[103] This refers to the ancient theory of the four humors, originated by Galen, and according to which the human body is composed of a balance of blood, phlegm, black bile, and yellow bile.

lowered from the bed, taken to the mortuary, and a short time after to the cemetery.

Poor boy! I was moved by his misfortune, and I wished I had never met him. He proved by his pen to be a man of average and decent principles, but he was guided by parents who were too indulgent, and for this reason, very pernicious.

They taught him that he could always get his way; they encouraged his arrogance and vanity; they did not instruct him in the principles of our holy religion; they raised an ungrateful son, a useless citizen, a pernicious man, and, perhaps at this very hour, a tormented spirit; but they too will have paid for their indolence in the same place where Don Catrín will pay for his outrageous immorality. Poor parents! How much better it would have been for these and so many others not to have children, if these were to grow up to be bad, as the infallible truth says.

Once I had read poor Don Catrín's notebooks, heard his conversations, and become aware of his way of thinking and his conscience, I felt sorry for him. I did my best to bring him around to the eternal truth, but it was too late; his heart was as hardened as the Pharaoh's.

I vowed to conclude the story of his life; but how should I stay true to the obligations of a faithful historian except by telling the truth and veiling nothing? And the truth is that he lived badly, died the same way, and left us with great grief and without any hope of his future happiness.

Even in this world, he had already begun to savor the fruits of his disordered conduct. Under the pretext of being wellborn, he tried to mirror the decency and proportions that he lacked and could never have obtained, for he was a staunch enemy of work. Slothfulness reduced him to the depths of misery, which brought him to prostitute himself through the most shameful of crimes.

He befriended the libertines and became one of them. His head was a repository of error and vanity: adorned with these beautiful qualities, he was ever impious, ignorant, and proud, making himself a thousand times insufferable and not a few times ridiculous.

His acts are the clearest testimony of his great talent, genteel education, and well-ordered conduct.

His whole life was an unceasing circle of disappointment, poverty, illness, humiliation, and disparagement; and in the prime of his life, death snatched his unhappy spirit away in the throes of the most agonizing remorse. He expired amidst disbelief, terror, and despair. Poor Catrín! May he have no imitators!

Upon his sepulchre, the following epitaph was engraved.

SONNET

The pride of his brethren, here lies Don Catrín,
Chivalrous gentleman of elevation,
Who sought distinction, luxury, and station
As a gambler, beggar, and marine.

For possessions and riches ever so keen,
Yet too dignified to take a vocation;
He stole, panhandled, and jeered at salvation.
Marvelous principles! Our staunch libertine!

Now he has parted without bidding farewell,
Leaving his devoted readers to surmise:
It was he who rang his untimely death knell.

Heed his story, Reader, until your last breath:
Those mortals who like Catrín live so unwell,
Will like Catrín suffer a similar death.

THE END OF DON CATRÍN DE LA FACHENDA

Works Cited in the Footnotes

Aylward, E. T. *Cervantes: Pioneer and Plagiarist*. Tamesis, 1982.

The Bible. New International Version, Biblica, 1984.

Frye, David L. Translator's Note. *The Mangy Parrot: The Life and Times of Periquillo Sarniento: Written by Himself for His Children*, translated by Frye, Hackett, 2004, pp. xxxi–xl.

Gay, Peter. *The Enlightenment: An Interpretation: The Rise of Modern Paganism*. W. W. Norton, 1966. Vol. 1 of *The Enlightenment: An Interpretation*.

Gonzalbo Aizpuru, Pilar. "Órden, educación y mala vida en la Nueva España." *Historia mexicana*, vol. 63, no. 1, 2013, pp. 7–50.

González Obregón, Luis. *Época colonial: México viejo, noticias históricas, tradiciones, leyendas y costumbres*. Librería Viuda de C. Bouret, 1900.

"Machiavellian." *Merriam-Webster*, 2021, www.merriam-webster.com/dictionary/Machiavellian.

Marrero-Fente, Raúl. "*Don Catrín de la Fachenda*: La ironía como expresión de una norma vacilante." *Acta Literaria*, no. 28, 2003, pp. 107–21.

Martínez Barbosa, Xóchitl. *El hospital de San Andrés: La evolución de la asistencia, la enseñanza y la investigación médicas en México*. Siglo Veintiuno Editores, 2005.

Olvarría y Ferrari, Enrique de. *Teatro en México*. 2nd ed., vol. 1, La Europea, 1895.

Spell, Jefferson Rea. "The Educational Views of Fernández de Lizardi." *Hispania*, vol. 9, no. 5, 1926, pp. 259–74.

Wasserman, Mark. *Everyday Life and Politics in Nineteenth Century Mexico: Men, Women, and War*. U of New Mexico P, 2000.